Book Seven

EPIC ZERO 7

Tales of a Long Lost Leader

By

R.L. Ullman

But That's
Another Story...
Press

Cover design and character illustrations by Yusup Mediyan.

Published by But That's Another Story... Press
Ridgefield, CT

Printed in the United States of America.

First Printing, 2020.

ISBN: 978-1-7340612-8-4
Library of Congress Control Number: 2020917415

For Howie & Sadie,
you came at the right time

BOOKS BY R.L. ULLMAN

EPIC ZERO SERIES

EPIC ZERO:
Tales of a Not-So-Super 6th Grader

EPIC ZERO 2:
Tales of a Pathetic Power Failure

EPIC ZERO 3:
Tales of a Super Lame Last Hope

EPIC ZERO 4:
Tales of a Total Waste of Time

EPIC ZERO 5:
Tales of an Unlikely Kid Outlaw

EPIC ZERO 6:
Tales of a Major Meta Disaster

EPIC ZERO 7:
Tales of a Long Lost Leader

EPIC ZERO 8:
Tales of a Colossal Boy Blunder

MONSTER PROBLEMS SERIES

MONSTER PROBLEMS:
Vampire Misfire

MONSTER PROBLEMS 2:
Down for the Count

MONSTER PROBLEMS 3:
Prince of Dorkness

TABLE OF CONTENTS

ONE

I DISPLAY MY MAD SKILLS

If things go according to plan this should be awesome.

Ten minutes ago, I got an alert from the Meta Monitor about a break-in at the Keystone City Museum. That gives us approximately seven minutes to beat the Freedom Force to the scene of the crime. They won't be expecting us, but I guess that's the advantage of being a member of two superhero teams. When evil flares up, I now have twice the chance of snuffing it out first.

Fortunately, we were already in the neighborhood eating ice cream a few blocks away. And since the Freedom Force will be dropping in from outer space, we'll easily get the jump on them. Boy, I can't wait to see Grace's face when she realizes we've already put the bad guy in handcuffs. I just hope someone gets it on camera.

But what'll be even better is if Dad is with them. Because if he is, then it will be the first time the leader of the Freedom Force and the leader of Next Gen showed up for the very same mission. And who is that brave, devilishly handsome new leader of Next Gen?

Oh yeah, that's me.

Truthfully, I still can't believe I've got my very own superhero team. I take in the faces of my teammates running beside me. All of them are focused. Determined. Ready to show the world what we can do. I can just see Dad looking at me with pride and saying something profound like—

"I've gotta go wee-wee."

Um, what?

"Seriously, Pinball?" Skunk Girl says. "Like, now?"

"I can't hold it," Pinball says, bouncing to a stop behind us. "I drank a whole milkshake before that alert came in. Can you guys just wait a sec? I don't know this area of town very well." Then, he bounds off into the nearest alley.

"But the bad guy will get away!" I call out, but it's no use. I run my hands through my hair. Well, there goes our time advantage. Now we'll never beat the Freedom Force to the scene. Sometimes I wonder why I bother getting out of bed.

"I knew we shouldn't have stopped for ice cream," Selfie says. "His bladder is even smaller than his brain."

Just then, I hear a tinkling sound to my left, and when I look down Dog-Gone is relieving himself on an unfortunate fire hydrant.

"You too, huh?" I say. "What a surprise."

This couldn't have happened at a worse time because this was our big chance to establish ourselves. I mean, if the Meta community is going to take us seriously we'll have to prove ourselves on the battlefield, not in the bathroom.

And so far our track record is less than stellar.

To date, our first and only real mission as a formal team was against Erase Face and that was almost a complete disaster. Erase Face is a Meta 1 villain who can erase things for good with his nose. I warned the team not to approach him head-on, but that didn't stop Skunk Girl from nearly losing her fingers, or Pinball from nearly losing his backside. Thank goodness for Selfie who blinded Erase Face with her magic phone while I neutralized his powers.

And Erase Face is only a Meta 1!

Since this mission will be far more dangerous maybe Pinball's bladder issue is a sign. Maybe we should pack up and go home before things get out of hand. After all, the Meta Monitor identified the perpetrator as a Meta 2.

"So, boss-man," Skunk Girl says, tapping her foot impatiently, "while we're waiting for pin-head can you run through this creep's background again?"

"Sure," I say, picturing his Meta profile in my mind.

"His name is Lunatick, and he's a Meta 2 Energy Manipulator with a toxic bite. He once was an archaeologist specializing in Egyptian ruins, but during one of his excavations, he was bitten by a strange, radioactive tick. The tick's venom took over his system, turning him into a Meta 2 bad guy with eight legs and a radioactive bite. Over time, the venom also messed with his mind, making him certifiably nuts. Hence, the name Luna-tick, as in 'Lunatic.' He's unpredictable, so let's try to be more careful this time."

"Understood," Skunk Girl says, flexing her fingers.

"Okay," Pinball says, bouncing out of the alley. "Sorry about that. You know, I really need to put a zipper in this costume."

"TMI," Selfie says. "Now let's go. We've lost a lot of time."

We take off again, but in my mind, we've 'lost' way more than time, because I'm betting the Freedom Force is already on the scene.

As we round the corner onto Main Street, I spot the Keystone City Museum in the distance. It's a large building that sort of looks like a giant seashell, with a domed roof and smooth, curved sides. But the impressive exterior isn't what has my attention, because I'm focused on the huge hole near the entrance where dozens of museumgoers are streaming outside.

"I think we're the first ones here," Selfie says. "I don't even see the police."

I scan the area and realize she's right. There aren't any cops, and more importantly, there aren't any heroes either. So, that means we still have a chance! But we've got to act fast.

"Follow me!" I yell. "And no more stopping!"

We race past the panicked crowd and through the large hole into the museum's cavernous entrance hall. That's when we see two security guards lying on the ground—and they're not moving.

"They're still breathing," Selfie says, checking on them. "They're just unconscious."

That's great news but I'm not surprised they're down for the count. I mean, Lunatick is a dangerous character. But when I scan the place there's no one around except for us and a giant Woolly Mammoth statue. Where did Lunatick go?

"What now?" Pinball asks, looking around. "Last year my class took a field trip here and this museum is ginormous. There's like a hall for everything."

I grab a map off the front desk and study it. It's been a while since I've been to the museum, but I know Pinball is right. There's a Hall of Meteorites, a Hall of Ocean Life, a Hall of American Mammals, and so much more. Where do we start? And why is Lunatick even here?

"Hey, look up," Selfie says, pointing to a large banner hanging from the ceiling. "This museum has a temporary exhibit of King Totenhotem's Tomb! And according to the banner, it opened today."

King Totenhotem's Tomb? King Tot? I remember studying King Tot in social studies class. He was an Egyptian kid pharaoh who died under mysterious circumstances. I stare at the giant image of King Tot's face and then look down at my map.

Then, everything clicks.

"This way!" I say, taking off to our right.

"Where are you going?" Skunk Girl calls out.

"To the Hall of Ancient Egypt," I say. "That's where King Tot's exhibit is located. Lunatick was an archaeologist, remember? I bet he's after something there. Now let's, um, squash that bug!"

Note to self: One thing I desperately need to do is come up with a good battle cry for our team. Before a fight, Dad always yells: "Freedom Force—It's Fight Time!" I tried using it for us, but it just didn't seem right. We need our own battle cry, but at the moment I've got nothing even close to that good.

To get to the Hall of Ancient Egypt, we first have to pass through the Hall of Biodiversity and its garden of rare plants, the Hall of Jurassic Dinosaurs and its giant T-Rex statue (which nearly gives me PTSD by the way), and the Hall of Meteorites with its giant map of the solar system. Then, we book down a flight of steps, swing around a corner, and find ourselves standing in front of the Hall of Ancient Egypt.

Over the door is a banner that reads: *King Tot Exhibit: Treasure of the Golden Kid Pharaoh. Ticket Holders Only.*

"He must be in there," I whisper. "Let's go inside."

"But we can't," Pinball whispers back, pointing to the sign. "We don't have tickets."

"Skunk Girl," I say, "feel free to slap him silly."

"Noted," she says.

"Now follow me," I say, "and remember, he's dangerous." I tiptoe through the entrance into a large chamber filled with hundreds of solid gold artifacts displayed inside glass cases. There are gold animal statues, gold musical instruments, gold dishware, and loads of other gold objects. As I pass through I realize this exhibit must be worth an absolute fortune.

But surprisingly, none of it looks disturbed. For some reason, Lunatick didn't want any of this stuff.

GRRRR.

I turn to find Dog-Gone staring at the statue of a life-sized, gold cat.

"Quiet," I whisper, clamping his muzzle shut. It's times like these I wish dogs came with a mute button.

Then, I notice there's another doorway on the far side of the room. A plaque above the entrance reads: *King Tot's Royal Sarcophagus*. Lunatick has to be in there.

I signal to the rest of the team and they nod. This is a time for maximum stealth. We got lucky he didn't hear Dog-Gone the first time, so now we've got to—

CRASH!

What was that? I spin around to find Pinball standing next to a tipped garbage can.

"Sorry," he whispers. "It didn't see me coming."

Just. Freaking. Wonderful.

Well, so much for the element of surprise.

"Okay, Next Gen," I say. "There's no hiding us now. Let's rock!"

"Let's *rock*?" Skunk Girl repeats dryly. "Can't you be more original than that?"

"I'll work on it later," I say. "Right now, we've got to focus on the task at—"

THOOM!

But before we can reach the next room, a bizarre insect-man bursts through the entranceway and lands directly in front of us! It's Lunatick, and he's way bigger than I expected! His round, insect body is wider than a refrigerator, and his swollen, human face stares at us with surprise. Then, I notice he's holding a golden staff in one of his eight legs, and the staff ends in the shape of an Egyptian ankh. That's King Tot's staff!

"Drop the artifact!" I command. "You're under arrest!"

"Well, what do we have here?" Lunatick says, seemingly amused by our presence. "Is the museum holding a preschool costume party?"

"Not funny," I reply, "and, well, actually rather insulting. No, we're Next Gen, and we're taking you down."

"I really don't have time for this," Lunatick says, jumping up and sticking to the ceiling. "So, if you'll excuse me, I'll just be crawling on my way now."

"Okay, team," I say, "here's the plan." But before I can utter another word, Pinball blurts out—

"I've got him!" And then he inflates his body into a giant ball and bounces up towards Lunatick.

"Pinball!" I yell. "Look—"

But Lunatick rears back and swats Pinball with the staff like he was backhanding a tennis ball.

"—out!" I finish.

"Duck!" Selfie yells as Pinball careens all over the room, shattering exhibit after exhibit until he finally wedges face-first into a display case!

"Help!" his muffled voice calls out. "I'm stuck!"

Something tells me this little outing just got more expensive than my piggy bank can afford.

"My turn!" Skunk Girl says, aiming her hands at Lunatick. But as her obnoxious scent hits Lunatick's nostrils it has the opposite effect of what was intended.

"My, that is delightful," Lunatick says, dropping to the ground and inhaling deep. "Perhaps you can bottle that fragrance for me and I can take it to go?" Then, he smashes through a display case, pulls out a gold vase, and flings it at Skunk Girl, hitting her hard on the shoulder.

Skunk Girl collapses in a heap.

"Skunk Girl!" Selfie cries, rushing to her side.

Well, this mission has quickly spiraled out of control, just like the last one. If I don't put an end to it now someone could get seriously hurt.

But when I turn to face Lunatick, he's gone! And so is Dog-Gone! I just catch the tip of his tail before he bolts out of the room after Lunatick.

"Dog-Gone, wait!"

But not surprisingly, he doesn't listen either.

"Selfie, help the others!" I say. "I'll get Lunatick!"

I race out of the room but Lunatick and Dog-Gone are long gone. Fortunately, they left a clear trail to follow! I climb back up the stairs and race through a huge hole in the Hall of Meteorites where Mars used to be, past a pile of T-Rex bones in the Hall of Jurassic Dinosaurs, and over several trampled rare plant species in the Hall of Biodiversity. Seconds later, I'm back in the entrance hall where I find Dog-Gone playing tug-of-war with Lunatick over the golden staff!

"Let go!" Lunatick yells, pulling at the staff with four legs. "I've spent my life searching for King Tot's tomb and this staff is worth a fortune on the black market! I'm not going to let some stupid mutt take it from me!"

But Dog-Gone doesn't yield and drops lower to the ground to gain more leverage.

"I warned you!" Lunatick says. "Now come closer and I'll show you what a real bite feels like!" Then, he opens his mouth, which is glowing with green energy, and reaches for Dog-Gone with two of his other legs!

"Dog-Gone!" I yell, but I'm too far away!

Lunatick is going to sink his toxic teeth into Dog-Gone! I'm about to negate his radioactive toxins when—

"Did someone call for an exterminator?" comes a familiar girl's voice.

Suddenly, a crimson streak flashes through the museum entrance and CRASHES into Lunatick, sending him flying. Lunatick SLAMS into the wall hard and sticks to the surface. Then, Grace lands next to me.

"Needed some help, huh?" she says, putting her arm around my shoulder.

That's when I notice Lunatick isn't holding the staff anymore. Dog-Gone has it!

"Fools!" Lunatick yells. "That artifact is mine!"

"I don't think so," comes a booming voice.

I turn to see Dad standing in the entranceway, flanked by the Freedom Force! "That staff belongs to the King Tot Foundation."

Great. We ran out of time before we could get the job done. Some leader I am.

"Now, you can either make this easy and surrender," Dad says, "or things could get ugly."

Just then, the rest of my team shows up.

"Wow, it's the Freedom Force!" Selfie says.

"Um, are you really Glory Girl?" Pinball asks Grace, staring at her wide-eyed with his jaw hanging open.

"Yeah," I say. "It's her. Why are you flipping out?"

"Never!" Lunatick responds to Dad.

"I was hoping you'd say that," Dad says, cracking his knuckles. "Freedom Force—It's Fight Time!"

"Now that's what a cool battle cry sounds like,"

Skunk Girl says, jabbing me in the arm.

***

Less than a minute later, the Freedom Force has wrapped everything up. Master Mime has Lunatick in four pairs of energy handcuffs, TechnocRat is tending to Skunk Girl's shoulder, and I'm sitting on the floor with the rest of my team wondering what went wrong. At least Dog-Gone was a hero today, although we can't even take credit for that because he hasn't officially joined our team.

So, I'd say this was pretty much an epic failure.

"Epic Zero," Dad calls from across the room. "Can we talk to you for a minute?"

And now I suspect it's about to get even worse.

"First of all, are you okay?" Dad asks as I approach.

"Yeah," I say. "I'm fine."

"Great," Dad says. "Lunatick is a Meta 2 villain, but I'm guessing you knew that, right?"

"Well, yeah," I say, looking at my feet.

"And your team has very little combat experience," Mom says. "Didn't you think this was more than you could handle? You're lucky Skunk Girl's injury wasn't more serious."

"I… I…," I stammer.

"Not to mention half the museum is destroyed," Dad adds. "Most of these things are irreplaceable."

"Yeah, I know," I say. "But Lunatick was—"

"—a dangerous villain," Dad says. "Too dangerous for your team to handle alone."

"Well, I… I mean, we…," I mutter.

Then, Mom and Dad exchange one of those looks that tells me they're having a private, telepathic conversation. And more often than not, those conversations end badly for me.

"Captain?" Blue Bolt calls out from across the room. "Can you look at this?"

"Coming," Dad says.

"We'll continue this later," Mom says.

"Yeah, fine," I say, slinking back over to my friends.

"What was that about?" Selfie asks.

"Oh, nothing good," I say. "Nothing good at all."

TWO

I RECEIVE SOME VERY BAD NEWS

There's nothing worse than waiting for the ax to fall.

I mean, it's been hours since my debacle at the Keystone City Museum. Of course, I offered to help with the cleanup but they said it would be best if my team and I went home. So, we said our goodbyes and now here I am, pacing anxiously on the Waystation 2.0 waiting for my parents to get back so we can finish our conversation.

The good news is Dad just got home after putting Lunatick in Lockdown. And Mom is on her way after working with the museum curators to assess all the damage we caused. Which means I know where my allowance will be going for the next hundred years.

I have so much on my mind I'd love to be alone.

But unfortunately, I'm not.

"So, wa' argh you gettin' merf for mye berfday?" Grace asks, talking with a mouth full of jelly doughnut.

"Um, what?" I say, barely catching a word.

"Holf on," she says, downing a glass of milk and wiping her chin with her sleeve. "I said, what are you getting me for my birthday? I'm turning fifteen in just a few days, remember? I'm expecting a big gift from you. Just a birthday card isn't going to cut it anymore."

"What?" I say, shocked we're even talking about this right now. "I don't know. Look, I'm a little preoccupied at the moment."

"Still thinking about your huge museum disaster, huh?" she says with a wry smile. "You screwed up. It happens."

"Gee, thanks," I say. "I know I screwed up, but I'm worried Mom and Dad aren't going to let this go. I think they might try to break up my team."

"For sure," Grace says, getting ready to take another bite of jelly doughnut. "You're all in over your heads."

"We are not!" I snap back.

"Seriously?" Grace says, looking at me like I have three heads. "Don't be a dufus and face the facts. You led an inexperienced team against a dangerous Meta 2 villain. What did you think would happen?"

"I… well, I…," I stammer. But truthfully, I don't have a great answer. I mean, she's right, what did I think would happen? Maybe I was being irresponsible.

"Now, let's get back to something more important," she says. "Like, what are you getting me for my birthday?"

"Elliott," comes Dad's voice over the intercom system, "please meet your mother and me in the Mission Room."

"Great," I say. "Well, I guess you can have my room for your birthday because apparently, I won't be needing it anymore."

"Awesome," she says. "I'll use it as a walk-in closet."

"Go for it," I say, heading into the hallway toward the Mission Room. As I walk, I feel like a prisoner heading for death row. I mean, based on Dad's stern tone, there's no way I'll escape without some kind of punishment. But I'll serve any sentence as long as they don't ask me to disband Next Gen.

Suddenly, something cold and wet nuzzles into my palm. "Hey, Dog-Gone," I say. "It's been nice knowing you. I hope you find a new master who isn't such a screw-up. Maybe try Shadow Hawk. He's got his act together."

Dog-Gone whimpers as I reach the Mission Room and see Mom and Dad sitting inside. "Stay out here, old boy," I say to Dog-Gone. "You don't want to see this."

Then, I go inside to face the music.

"Have a seat, son," Dad says, his expression serious.

As I plop into one of the chairs around the circular conference table, I glance at Mom to judge her demeanor but she looks just as serious as Dad. So, this is gonna be bad. As Dad opens his mouth, I brace myself for what's to come.

"Elliott," Dad says, "we want to have a conversation with you about leadership."

What? Did he just say they want to have a conversation with me about leadership? Seriously? That's it? "Um, sure," I say, sitting up straighter. "Great. Let's converse then. I love conversing."

"Being a leader is a big job," Dad says. "And at its core are two fundamental responsibilities. The first, of course, is accomplishing the mission at hand. But the second is less obvious but equally important, and that's looking out for the welfare of your team. In our business, we deal with life and death situations, and a leader must quickly assess if his or her team is even capable of handling the mission. And if the answer is 'no,' the leader must protect the team from unnecessary harm. Do you understand what I'm saying?"

"Yeah," I say, nodding. "You're saying we bit off more than we could chew. But the Freedom Force takes on every mission. It's easy for you because you don't have to worry about the capabilities of your team."

"I'll let you in on a little secret," Dad says. "I'm always worried about our team. Even though we're all capable heroes who have worked together for years, we're constantly learning how to be a better team. We encounter new threats every day, and I never stop thinking about how we'll handle certain situations. It's part of being a leader. Feeling too comfortable can be your undoing."

"Okay, I get it," I say, crossing my arms. "So, is that it? Is that all you wanted to tell me?"

Mom and Dad look at one another.

"No," Mom says. "Elliott, we don't think Next Gen is ready for action. We think it's great that you have Meta friends, and we think it would be good for you to get together to practice every once in a while, maybe even here in the Combat Room, but it's just not safe for you to be out in the real world taking on real Meta criminals."

"That's not fair!" I shoot back. "You just told me the Freedom Force is constantly learning how to be a better team. That's no different than us."

"That's true," Mom says, "but we are all established heroes in our own right. Your friends are just kids who are still learning how to use their powers."

"Well, this kid has already saved the universe a few times," I say, pointing to myself. "You know, in case it slipped your minds."

"Elliott," Mom says, "we know that. And that's why you're a member of the Freedom Force. But being a part of *our* team and leading a team of inexperienced heroes is not the same thing."

"So, just to be clear," I say, "you're saying you don't think I'm a good enough leader?"

"We're saying that you're still an inexperienced

leader," Dad says. "Leadership is a skill that takes time to develop, and until you get more experience it's simply not safe for you and your friends to be developing your skills on the fly and in public. What if Lunatick had hit Skunk Girl in the head with that vase instead of her shoulder?"

"Well…," I mutter.

"Or what if the museum was filled with people when you confronted Lunatick?" Dad continues.

"Well, I guess, um," I sputter.

"Leaders need to think these scenarios through," Dad says, "often before they even happen. Elliott, you have all the potential in the world to be a great leader, but you and your friends are still kids. You need to practice in a safe environment."

I open my mouth to respond, but nothing comes out. Deep down I know he's probably right, but I don't want to tell him that.

"Are we done?" I ask.

"Almost," Mom says. "We would like you to officially disband Next Gen."

"What?" I say. "Really?"

"Really," Dad says. "We know this isn't what you wanted to hear, but it's the right thing to do for the safety of everyone involved. Then, when you guys are older, you can get the band back together again."

"Are we finished conversing?" I say, standing up.

"Elliott—," Mom starts.

"No, I got the message loud and clear," I say.

"Thanks for the pep talk."

"Elliott, please understand," Dad says.

But I'm so upset I can't respond. As I walk out of the Mission Room I find Dog-Gone still standing there. He looks at me with sad eyes and whimpers. "Not now," I say, brushing past him. My blood is boiling and I just want to get as far away from my parents as possible.

I mean, I can't believe they want me to disband Next Gen! How overprotective can you get? They're not even giving us a chance to show what we can do. It's not fair.

As I wander through the halls I can just picture the reaction of the team when I tell them the news. I can see them staring at me with disappointment on their faces. And who's to say they won't just continue without me? I mean, they were already a team before they asked me to join them. They'll probably just say goodbye to me and keep on fighting.

Not that I'm a big help anyway.

Grace was right, the mission was a disaster. And I hate to admit it, but if Grace didn't get there when she did, I could have lost Dog-Gone. Breaking up Next Gen is the last thing I want, but maybe it's for the best.

Just then, I nearly crash into a huge object blocking my path. What the—?

I look up to find a giant, yellow brain suspended in clear goo inside a glass tube. It's spongy and absolutely disgusting. For a second, I'm totally confused. Did I just get transported to an alien planet? But when I look around I realize what happened.

I wandered into the Trophy Room.

The Trophy Room is a section on the Waystation that collects all sorts of interesting—and sometimes dangerous—mementos from the Freedom Force's various missions. Ironically, I guess it's sort of like a museum itself, with hundreds of items on display. The Trophy Room used to be even larger, but what's here now is everything we were able to recover from space after the first Waystation was blown to smithereens thanks to me and the Meta-Busters.

I guess it's just another reminder of my failures as a Meta hero.

I look at the large brain floating in front of me and read the plaque beneath it: *Hive Mind of the Bee-lug Race (Alien)*. Interesting. I saunter through the chamber, looking at other fascinating artifacts like the *Battle Armor of Nikademis*, the *Sphere of Dark Matter*, the *4-D Ray Gun of Doom*, and the *Statue of Medusa IV*.

Then, something shiny catches my eye that I've never noticed before.

On a stand in the corner is a bronze signet ring beneath a glass cover. It's only when I get closer that I notice the symbol of a lightning bolt carved into its face. The plaque on the stand reads: *The Three Rings of Suffering. Extremely Dangerous. Do not remove from glass. DO NOT WEAR UNDER ANY CIRCUMSTANCES.*

The Three Rings of Suffering? What does that mean?

And what happened to the other two rings? Hopefully, they're not floating in outer space.

I stretch my arms and yawn. I should probably just go to bed. And based on what my parents want me to do, I'll need all the rest I can get. Not that I'm going to get any sleep anyway. After all, I have no idea how I'll break the news to my team without looking like a total loser.

Which, I'm guessing, will be impossible.

As I wander to my room I can't stop thinking about how I could prove my parents wrong. I mean, how can I show them that Next Gen is a great superhero team too? Unfortunately, nothing comes to mind. I just wish they would give us some space. And speaking of space, when I reach my door an unexpected visitor is waiting for me with his tail wagging.

"Okay, Dog-Gone," I say, opening the door. "You can sleep with me, but no hogging the covers."

I brush my teeth, put my mask and cape on my desk, and crawl into bed with my uniform still on. Dog-Gone hops onto the bed, circles around, and settles down on my legs, crushing them. Note to self: start a doggie diet plan tomorrow.

And as I drift off to sleep, there's only one thought floating through my brain:

Why do grown-ups get to make all the rules?

THREE

I WISH I STAYED IN BED

I wake up shivering.

I reach down to pull up my covers but they aren't there. What happened? But it's not until I roll over that I find my answer, because Dog-Gone is snoring blissfully by my side with his head on my pillow and his body wrapped snugly inside my blankets. Yep, I should have known better.

I rub my eyes and look at the clock. It's 6:01 a.m. which is way earlier than I wanted to get up. It would have been great to sleep in, but thanks to my slobbering bunkmate that's not going to happen. But I can't blame him for everything. After all, there's so much on my mind I was bound to have a restless sleep anyway.

I mean, I still don't know what I'm going to say to Next Gen. I must have woken up ten times sweating about it, and I still don't have a clue. The team is relying on me to lead them, and now I get to tell them we need to disband.

I can just see their reactions now. Pinball will be shocked, Selfie will be disappointed, and Skunk Girl will ask me some really tough questions—like if I'm also quitting the Freedom Force. And what's worse is I can already see her laughing at me when I tell her I'm not. So, this is pretty much a lose-lose situation.

Thanks, Mom and Dad.

But maybe if I'm just straightforward with them they'll understand. Maybe they'll get it if I tell them it's for our safety and the safety of those around us.

Then again, maybe I'm delusional.

I get out of bed, walk into the bathroom, and check myself in the mirror. My hair is messy, my eyes are puffy, and my skin is paler than a zombie. Well, I look far from confident, so they'll probably eat me alive.

And I'm pretty sure this will be the last time I see Selfie. I mean, I get this weird feeling in my stomach whenever I'm around her. But after she hears what I'm going to say she'll probably hate me forever.

I breathe in and exhale. This just might be the worst day of my life. And believe me, that's saying something. Well, I'd better fuel up with a good breakfast because it's going to be a long day. I exit the bathroom to find Dog-

Gone yawning by the door.

"Oh, did I disturb you?" I ask. "Gee, I'm so sorry."

But he just scratches his ear with his hind leg.

"C'mon," I say, grabbing my mask and cape. "I'll put you in the Evacuation Chamber and then we'll get something to eat."

I have to say, TechnocRat thought of almost everything when he designed the Waystation 2.0. Now, when Dog-Gone has to go to the bathroom, we put him in the Evacuation Chamber and push a button to eject his business into outer space where it'll burn up before it hits Earth's atmosphere. Sadly, based on what I need to tell Next Gen, I'm tempted to eject myself with it.

Anyway, once he's done we head to the Galley to find a distressed-looking Grace in her Glory Girl uniform frantically reading all the post-it notes on the refrigerator.

"You're up early," I say.

"Have you seen Mom or Dad?" she asks, ripping the notes down one by one.

"No," I say. "Are they in the Mission Room? Usually, they're up at five to catch the early news."

"Duh," Grace says. "I know what they usually do but they're not there. In fact, I can't find them anywhere and they didn't leave a note."

"Did you ask Blue Bolt or Shadow Hawk?" I ask, opening the cupboard to grab Dog-Gone's food.

"They're not here either," Grace says. "And neither are Master Mime, Makeshift, or TechnocRat."

"Really?" I say. Come to think of it, I haven't seen any of them either. "And there's no note?"

"No," Grace says. "I've checked everywhere. Dad was supposed to meet me in the Combat Room at six for a workout, but he never showed up."

"Well, that is weird," I say. Mom and Dad always leave a note if they go on a mission while we're sleeping. Suddenly, I get an uneasy feeling in my stomach.

I put down Dog-Gone's food and he starts crunching away. Where could they be? Just then, I remember that time when Leo kidnapped me and I wasn't able to leave a note. I wonder if they were adult-napped?

"I even had the Meta Monitor scan the Waystation for Meta readings," Grace says. "But there's nothing."

"Okay," I say. "That's not good. Did you see if there was anything big happening on the news?"

"No," Grace says. "Hand me the remote."

I pass her the remote control and she flicks on the big television near the table, but there's just static.

"Did you mess up the remote again?" she asks.

"No," I say. "I didn't touch it."

But as Grace clicks through, there's static on every channel. "This is ridiculous," she says. "Turn on the radio."

I flip on the radio, which is usually tuned into the news, but all we hear is a high-pitched beep. I change the station but it's the same thing. Every station has the same high-pitched beep.

"Something is wrong," Grace says, grabbing her phone off the counter. "There's no text messages either."

Okay, now I'm starting to worry. This is totally unlike Mom and Dad. Where did they go?

"Elliott!" Grace blurts out wide-eyed as she scrolls through her phone. "Look at this!"

"What?" I say, running over. "What is it?"

"Look!" she says. "Look at all these kids posting on social media. Their parents are missing too!"

As Grace scrolls through her newsfeed, I see all of these posts and videos from kids whose parents are missing. But it's not just the parents, but their older brothers and sisters too! And these posts are coming from all over the world!

"This is nuts!" Grace says. "According to these kids, anyone over the age of fifteen is gone!"

Gone? But gone where?

"Follow me," Grace says. "Let's see if we can figure out what's happening in the Mission Room."

As Dog-Gone and I chase her through the hallway I think back to last night when I was in the Mission Room with Mom and Dad. At the time I was so mad I just wanted to get away from them. But I didn't really mean it! I would never want anything bad to happen to them.

By the time we reach the Mission Room, Grace is already putting on a headset at the control panel.

"Freedom Force to White House," she says into the microphone. "White House, do you read me?"

But all we hear is static.

"Freedom Force to Keystone City Police," she tries next. "Anyone there? Hello? Hello?"

But there's nothing.

"No one is responding," Grace says.

"Are the vehicles still in the Hangar?" I ask. "Did they take a Freedom Flyer?"

"Good question," Grace says, and then she pushes a few buttons and a visual of the Hangar pops up on the main screen. "Nope," she says. "All of the vehicles are parked in their spots. Holy smokes!"

"What?" I ask. "Holy smokes what?"

"If anyone over fifteen just up and vanished," she says, typing into the keyboard, "then what about all of the vehicles that adults drive? Like cars, buses, and—"

"—planes!" I finish for her. "Do a scan!"

"Scanning," Grace says, typing away, and then up pops a list of flights in the air. Luckily, there are only three flights in service across the United States. "I'm on it," she says, hopping off her chair. "I'll take a Freedom Ferry and land them one by one. Do another scan and see what else you can turn up. And don't do anything stupid!"

But before I can respond she's gone. I hop into her chair and start punching into the keyboard. Based on the limited number of planes in the air, whatever happened must have taken place between midnight and six o'clock in the morning when most people are asleep. At least that might limit some of the damage.

Okay, let's take a look at the highway. I push some buttons and an image of the interstate appears. The good news is that no vehicles are moving. The bad news is that the ones I do see are crashed all over the place. Then, I remember the subway system. I press a few keys and a visual of the subway routing system appears. Fortunately, there aren't any cars on the tracks, which pretty much confirms this happened before the subway opened at six.

Now, what else do adults drive? Suddenly, I hear crunching and look over to find Dog-Gone still chewing his food. Wait, chewing? Chew. Choo Choo! Trains!

I punch in a few more commands and a map of the railroad system pops up. It's all clear, except for a massive freight train running along a stretch of track heading straight for Keystone City! And there's another train already parked at the terminal! They're gonna collide!

I've got to stop that train! But before I do I'm going to need help managing anything else that pops up. So, I type into the new transmitter watch I asked TechnocRat to develop for me and my team.

<Epic Zero: Team I need help! Everyone over 15 is gone! Go see if any kids need help on streets & highways!>

Five seconds later I get:

<Selfie: On it! My parents r gone too!>

<Skunk Girl: Roger and same! ☺>

<Pinball: Just need a sec 2 eat breakfast.>

Okay, great. While Pinball finishes his pancakes, I've

got a runaway train to catch! But before I go I've got one last thing to handle.

"Dog-Gone, stay," I order. "I'll be back in a bit."

But Dog-Gone growls in disagreement. Honestly, I don't have time to argue, and now that I think of it, maybe he should come along anyway. After all, who knows what kinds of trouble he'll get into if he stays here all by himself.

"Okay, okay," I say. "You can come, but you have to listen to everything I say. Is that a deal?"

Dog-Gone barks and we race for the Hangar.

***

Five minutes later, our Freedom Ferry touches down at the Keystone City Railroad Terminal. We hop out and make our way onto the tracks. Here's the parked train, but where's the—

CHUGACHUGACHUGA!

I spin around to see a massive train heading our way! Smoke is pouring out of the chimney and it doesn't seem like it's going to stop on its own. I've probably got a minute before it's here.

The only problem is that I didn't think this through. My powers don't work on inanimate objects, and other than Dog-Gone, there's no Metas around to duplicate.

So, now what?

Think, Elliott, think!

I look over at the Freedom Ferry. I guess we could get back inside and shoot it with a missile, but what if someone is on board? I mean, kids stowaway on trains all the time in the movies.

But as I look back at the train, I realize there's no time! In fact, that train is coming in way faster than I expected! It's nearly on top of us! I grab Dog-Gone's collar, but before we can move—

"Look out, kid!" comes a girl's voice.

Suddenly, a masked girl riding a black slide generated from her fingertips flies towards us. Then, she raises her other hand and shifts a shadow from the ground to right in front of us! The next thing I know, the shadow solidifies and arcs over our heads just as the train reaches us! But instead of crushing us, the train rides up the solid shadow and goes right over us!

THOOM!

I spin around as the runaway train drops on top of the parked train! I can't believe it. We're okay. The train didn't touch us at all!

Then, the girl rides her strange slide over to us.

"Are you okay?" she asks.

"Um, yeah," I say, kind of embarrassed. I mean, she probably just saved our lives. "Thanks for that."

"No problem," she says, with a slight smile.

She looks like she's about my age, with long, black hair and bright, brown eyes. Her costume is all black, except for the insignia on her top that looks like a small, gray owl.

"Um, why are you wearing that costume?" she asks. "I mean, you're dressed like a Meta but you sure didn't act like one."

"Oh," I say, my face feeling flush. "Well, I am a Meta but my powers didn't quite fit the situation. I'm Epic Zero."

Dog-Gone barks.

"And that's Dog-Gone," I add. "My dog."

Dog-Gone claws my leg.

"Ow!" I say, and when I look down at him he looks none too pleased with me. "And apparently he'd like you to know that he's a Meta too."

"I see," she says. "Nice to meet you. Well, you'd better be careful. All of the adults are missing which is why that train wasn't going to stop."

"Yeah, I know," I say. "And actually, it's anyone over fifteen."

"Really?" she says. "I didn't know that. I've been trying to help wherever I can but everything is nuts."

"Clearly," I say. "Are you new around here?"

"Yeah," she says. "You can say that. Well, I've got to go but here's a tip for you, don't stand in front of a runaway train. See ya."

Then, she generates another dark slide and takes off!

"Wait!" I call after her. "I never got your—"

But then she disappears over the terminal.

"—name."

Meta Profile

Lunatick

Name: Carter Jones	Height: 6'0"
Race: Humanoid	Weight: 390 lbs
Status: Villain/Active	Eyes/Hair: Brown/Brown

META 2: Energy Manipulator	Observed Characteristics	
Considerable Radioactive Bite	Combat 62	
Possesses the reflexes and wall-climbing abilities of a tick	Durability 44	Leadership 16
	Strategy 23	Willpower 64

FOUR

I GATHER THE TROOPS

I couldn't get away from there fast enough.

I mean, after thoroughly embarrassing myself with the mysterious masked girl at the train station, I was feeling pretty low. So, I grabbed Dog-Gone and jetted over to the Hangout to meet up with Next Gen. The Hangout is the name we gave our treehouse headquarters in Selfie's backyard. It's not as decked out as the Waystation 2.0, or even the Waystation 1.0 for that matter, but it's got all the basics for effective crime-fighting, including a police monitor, maps of the city, and plenty of snacks.

Since there's no one left on the planet with a driver's license, I park the Freedom Ferry in Selfie's driveway and head around back. Unfortunately, Dog-Gone is still afraid to climb the treehouse ladder, so I spend the next few minutes chasing him around the yard until I bribe him with cheese puffs. After pushing his rump up the ladder, we finally make it to the top where I find the rest of Next Gen watching us from above.

"Here," Selfie says, handing me the bag of cheese puffs. "I think he has you trained by now."

"Probably," I say, fishing out a few. Dog-Gone gobbles them up and looks at me with his orange-covered snout. "That's it. No more."

"That's what you said last time," Skunk Girl says. "And yet, here we are again."

"Anyway," I say, ignoring her. "What did you guys run into?"

"Craziness," Selfie says. "It's complete and utter craziness out there. Kids are running around town in packs. The older ones have collected the younger ones and are trying to feed them and keep them calm, but they're just kids themselves. Everyone is scared and everyone is looking for their parents. And the babies are the ones suffering the most. They're crying non-stop for food and no one is volunteering for diaper duty, if you catch my drift."

"I do," Skunk Girl says, raising her right arm. "But for some of us, being odoriferous is a good thing."

"Funny," Selfie says. "But we've got serious problems here. I mean, no one knows what happened to our parents or older siblings. There's panic out there and most of the kids are way too young to take care of themselves. And I'm not just talking about Keystone City. This is happening across the country, let alone the world!"

"It's nuts," Pinball says, leaning his round body against the squared-off corner. "I never realized how much we relied on adults. A toddler I was helping thought I was a watermelon and tried to bite me! Can you believe it? What were you up to, Epic Zero?"

Great question. I could tell them I was nearly run over by a freight train until a masked Meta-girl saved my bacon, but I'm not sure that would instill confidence in my leadership abilities. So, instead, I settle on—

"I, um, tried to prevent an accident at the railroad station."

"Speaking of accidents," Skunk Girl says. "There are, like, thousands of bashed up, stranded cars on the roads. It's like the aftermath of a giant demolition derby. Who's going to fix this mess?"

"We are," I say boldly.

"You've got that right, squirt," comes a familiar voice.

"Glory Girl?" Pinball says, his jaw hanging open. "W-What are you doing here?"

"He called me," Grace says, nodding at me as she floats through the entrance and touches down next to me. "So, is this really your headquarters?"

"Don't start," I say.

"H-Hey," Pinball says, sitting up straighter. "I'm Binpall, I mean, Pinbowl. I-I mean, Pinball. I'm a big fan of yours."

"Nice to meet you," Grace says.

"I'm Selfie," Selfie says, shaking Grace's hand. "We didn't introduce ourselves last time but it's a real honor to meet you."

"An honor?" I say, crossing my arms. "So, what am I? Chopped liver?"

"I'm Skunk Girl," Skunk Girl says, waving awkwardly.

"Yes, you are," Grace says, her nose twitching. Then, she looks at me and whispers, "So, did you tell them the bad news?"

"Shut it," I whisper back.

"You mean, you didn't tell them?" she asks.

"I said shut it," I reply.

"Tell us what?" Selfie asks.

"Absolutely nothing," I say quickly. Then, I give Grace a death stare and say, "It's just that now that there are no adults around, the things that some adults may have wanted before this situation happened are no longer valid because the adults aren't here. So, we're operating in an adult-free environment right now and everyone—and I mean everyone—needs to adapt accordingly."

"Okay, okay, relax," Grace says. "Under the 'adult-free' situation that's fine. But once we fix this we'll talk."

"Are people on the Freedom Force always this weird?" Skunk Girl asks Pinball.

"I hope so," Pinball says, staring at Grace with goo-goo eyes.

"What's his problem?" Grace asks, looking at Pinball.

"No one really knows," Selfie answers. "Anyway, you said we were the ones who were going to fix this. How are we going to do that?"

"Well, we've got three problems to solve," Grace says, grabbing the bag of cheese puffs from me. "One, we're out of jelly doughnuts on the Waystation. Two, we've got to find out what's happening. I mean, it's not every day that people over the age of fifteen disappear off the face of the Earth. Someone is responsible for this. The question is who? And why?"

Well, she's right about that. But as I think through all of the evil profiles in the Meta Monitor's database, I can't think of anyone powerful enough to pull off something like this.

"So," Grace continues, shoving a cheese puff into her mouth, "after I safely landed all three airplanes I went back to the Waystation and asked the Meta Monitor to identify any strange Meta readings."

"And?" I ask.

"Bupkus," she says, eating another cheese puff.

"Great," I say.

"The third problem," Grace says, "is how are we

going to govern society until we can get the adults back? I mean, think about it. Who's in charge of the country right now? No one. There's no president, vice president, or Congress. There's no army, no air force, and no police protecting us. No one is producing or selling food. There aren't any doctors, nurses, or even dentists. Well, maybe that last one is a blessing, but you get the point. It's a kids' world now."

"That's a great summary," Skunk Girl says, "but what are we going to do about it? I mean, we're just kids ourselves."

"True," Grace says, gobbling the last cheese puff. "We're kids but we're not ordinary kids. We're Meta kids and we've got to step up."

"Exactly," I say. "That's what I was trying to tell them when you showed—"

"So, here's the plan," Grace says, cutting me off and handing me the empty bag. "It's up to us to run the nation. So, effective immediately, I'll be taking the role of President of the United States of America."

"Wait, what?" I say.

"Yep," she says, "we need someone to lead the country. And as a Meta and member of the Freedom Force, I'm the only logical choice."

"Um, sorry to remind you," I say, "but I'm also a Meta and member of the Freedom Force."

"True," Grace says, "but I'm the senior-ranking member of the Freedom Force. And besides, the people need a face they can trust. Plus, I'm more popular."

"That's great for you," I say, "but running the country isn't about getting brand sponsorship deals. It's about making smart decisions for the people. Besides, you can't just claim the presidency. Normally there's, like, a whole election process, remember?"

"These aren't normal times," Grace says matter-of-factly. "This is a time for swift action."

"Well, I'd vote for her," Pinball says.

"See, there you go," Grace says, heading for the exit. "I've just been elected. Now, I'm heading to the White House to get our government up and running. In the meantime, I need you guys to help guide and protect my citizens while I search for the culprit."

"*My* citizens?" I say. "Look, you can't be serious."

"As you said, we're operating in an 'adult-free environment,'" Grace says, looking me dead in the eyes. "And *everyone* needs to adapt accordingly. Otherwise, someone's beans may be spilled. Capeesh?"

We stare at each other for a few seconds.

"Capeesh," I say reluctantly. "But, um, aren't you forgetting something?"

"What's that?" she says, stopping at the ladder.

"Well, you turn fifteen in a few days," I say. "So, if we don't figure this out fast, you'll be the shortest tenured president in American history."

Grace's smile fades and I see the concern in her eyes.

"Then we'd better get to work as soon as possible,"

she says, and then she steps off the platform and flies away.

"Goodbye, Madame President!" Pinball calls out.

"Well, this should be interesting," Selfie says.

"Oh, you have no idea," I answer.

Honestly, the thought of a 'President Grace' doesn't leave me feeling warm and fuzzy. I mean, this is the girl who spends more time in front of a mirror than a newspaper. But she's right, someone needs to get the government running. And even though she's my annoying big sister, I trust her to do the right thing. Plus, there's so much to do right now it's not productive to squabble over who does what.

But what's worse than President Grace is no Grace at all. So, we've got to solve this mystery before her birthday. I can't have her disappearing on me too.

"What now, boss?" Skunk Girl asks.

I turn to find the team looking at me like I've actually got an answer. I smile as my mind goes into overdrive. Truthfully, I have no idea what to do next. According to our self-elected new president, it's up to us to guide and protect the public.

But if we're going to do that, we're gonna need a lot of help because it's a big country out there. If only there were more of us. Then, we could all join forces and become the next Freedom F—

Wait a second. That's it!

My parents wanted me to disband Next Gen, but

desperate times call for desperate measures!

"Um, are you okay?" Selfie asks. "You've got a strange look on your face."

"What?" I say. "Oh, sorry. Didn't you tell me that you guys met in a chat room or something like that?"

"Yeah," Pinball says. "It's called the Freedom Force Kids Forum. There are lots of kids in there who are fans of the Freedom Force. But once the three of us found each other, we sort of started chatting on our own. That's when we realized we all had Meta powers."

"Interesting," I say. "So, if you guys were in that chat room, then maybe there are other Meta kids in there too."

"Um, sorry but I'm totally confused," Skunk Girl says. "Why are we talking about chat rooms right now? Where are you going with this?"

"I'm thinking big," I say, "because if we're going to guide and protect the country, we're going to need a larger squad."

"Wait," Selfie says. "Are you saying we need a bigger team?"

"Yep," I say. "That's why we're going to hold our first-open audition to recruit new members for Next Gen!"

FIVE

I HOLD AN AUDITION

The turnout is way bigger than I expected.

I mean, Pinball posted our superhero tryout in the Freedom Force Kids Forum only a few hours ago, but apparently, word got around quick because every seat in the Keystone Middle School auditorium is taken. I'm standing on the stage with the rest of the team marveling at the large crowd. There must be a hundred kids here who want to try out for Next Gen!

I haven't felt this pumped in a while. This is, without a doubt, the best call I've made as team leader so far. I glance over at Selfie who smiles at me. Yep, Grace can be president for all I care, I'm happy right where I am.

Now, I don't like to toot my own horn, but I'm pretty sure most of these kids are here because of me.

After all, I asked Pinball to include in his post that Next Gen isn't led by just any Meta hero, but by a bona fide member of the Freedom Force. I thought it might be a draw, but maybe it worked too well. The place is so packed it'll take hours to get through the auditions.

"Excuse me," calls a little girl with her hand in the air. She's sitting in the front row and can't be older than nine. I wonder what her powers are.

"Yes," I say, kneeling. She probably wants my autograph but that'll have to wait. In fact, maybe I'll do an autograph signing for everyone at the end of the audition. I just hope my hand doesn't cramp.

"Is Glory Girl late?" the little girl asks.

"Glory Girl?" I say, confused. "Um, no, she's not part of our team."

"Oh," the little girl says, her face falling with disappointment. "The post said Glory Girl was in charge of Next Gen."

"It said what?" I say, looking over at Pinball.

"Well," Pinball says, turning bright red, "you weren't very specific. You told me to say the team was led by a member of the Freedom Force. So, I, um, kinda said Glory Girl was in charge. But it's sort of true, right? I mean, she is the president and all."

"Glory Girl may be the president," I say, "but I'm the leader of Next Gen. Not Glory Girl."

"Where are the chips and salsa?" a boy calls out from the back of the auditorium. "The post said there would be chips and salsa."

Chips and salsa?

I glare at Pinball again.

"Well," Pinball says, his rotund stature somehow shrinking. "I, um, sort of said we'd be serving free chips and salsa too."

"You said what?" Skunk Girl says, slapping her palm against her forehead. "We're not serving chips and salsa! We don't even have chips and salsa! Why would you say something like that?"

"Because I, um, didn't think anyone would show up otherwise," Pinball says, shuffling uncomfortably on his feet. "I didn't want it to be just us."

"Holy smokes," Selfie says, running her hands through her hair. "So, that means none of these kids have Meta powers."

"I'm hungry!" a boy calls out.

"Me too!" another boy says.

Suddenly, the whole crowd starts complaining and the volume level rises until I can't even think straight anymore. This has gotten out of control!

"Everyone, please stay calm!" I shout out to the crowd. "Can I get your attention please?"

It takes a few seconds for the auditorium to quiet down, but when it does I say, "I'm sorry to make this announcement, but despite what the post said, Glory Girl is not in charge of Next Gen and we are not serving chips and salsa. I repeat we are not serving chips and salsa. The only people who should be here are those kids who have Meta powers and want to try out for Next Gen, our superhero team. If you are not one of those people then please exit the auditorium in a calm and orderly manner."

There, that should do it.

But then the complaining starts all over again.

"There's no chips and salsa?"

"Glory Girl isn't here?"

"You stink, Epic Zebra!"

Well, so much for my autograph session. As the crowd stands up and files out of the auditorium, I bury my face in my hands and try to take calming breaths. Note to self: fire Pinball as head of our public relations department.

"Epic Zero," Selfie whispers, elbowing me in the ribs. "Look!"

What now? But when I look up I'm shocked, because three kids are still sitting in their seats. And they're all wearing costumes! They must be real Metas!

"See," I say to the team, perking up again. "I told you it would work out." Then, I look at our three candidates and say, "Welcome! Thank you so much for coming. Why don't we get off the stage and we'll hand it over to you so you can show us what you can do."

We take our seats in the front row as the three kids make their way up to the stage. There are two boys and a girl who all look about our age. This is exciting. I just hope they're good enough to make the cut.

"This should be entertaining," Pinball says. "Boy, I sure wish we brought chips and salsa."

"Shut it," Skunk Girl says.

"Okay," I say. "Who would like to go first?"

"I'll go," one of the boys offers, moving to center stage. He's tall and thin, with red hair and freckles on his nose and cheeks. His blue eyes shift nervously in his red mask and he's wearing a red costume with a blue-and-orange 'T' on the front.

"Thanks for volunteering," I say, wishing I had something to take notes with. "What's your name?"

"I call myself Thermo," he says.

"Nice to meet you, Thermo," I say. "And thanks for coming down to audition for Next Gen. As of, well, this morning, we became the premier superhero team on the planet. So, to join us you'll really need to knock our capes off. Are you ready to show us what you can do?"

"Oh, I already have," he says, furrowing his brow.

"Um, is something happening I'm not seeing?" Skunk Girl whispers after a few seconds. "Because I'm not seeing him do anything."

Just then, Selfie shudders and crosses her arms. "W-Why is it so c-cold in here all of a s-sudden?"

One second later, my skin starts feeling numb and my teeth begin to chatter! Selfie is right, it's absolutely freezing in here. And when I exhale I can see my breath rise in front of my face as wispy puffs of vapor! "A-A-Are y-y-you d-d-doing th-th-this?" I stammer.

"Too cold in here for you?" Thermo asks, raising his eyebrows. "Don't worry, I can change that."

Suddenly, the frigid chill fades, only to be replaced by thick, oppressive humidity! In fact, it's so unbearably warm I just want to tear off my costume and jump in a swimming pool! I look over at Dog-Gone who is lying on the floor with his tongue hanging out, panting like crazy.

"This is... getting ridiculous," Skunk Girls says, breathing hard and pulling down the fur neckline of her costume.

"C-Can't breathe," Pinball says. His cheeks are red and sweat is pouring down his face.

"O-Okay," I say. "Please, stop!"

"Certainly," Thermo says, relaxing his expression.

Just then, the temperature returns to normal.

"Thank goodness," Selfie says, wiping her brow.

"Well, I'm impressed," I say. And I really am. I mean, my body literally felt like it was put through the wringer. This kid has unique powers that could be useful. "So, how long have you had the ability to control the temperature?"

"For a year or so," Thermo says. "I realized I could do it at school when I was trying to get out of a math test. I shut the whole air conditioning system down."

"Well, that might be the best use of a power I've ever heard of," I say. "But have you ever used it in battle?"

"No," Thermo says. "I can only do it indoors where there's a thermostat system to connect to. My powers don't work outside."

"Wait, did you just say your powers don't work outside?" Pinball repeats. "Like, not at all?"

"No," Thermo says. "But I'm an orange belt in karate so I can chop some people if you need me to."

"Riiight," I say. Suddenly, I'm feeling much less enthusiastic about Thermo. I mean, I can't think of too many battles I've fought in the comfort of air conditioning. "Thank you. We'll, um, make our decisions at the end of all of the auditions. For now, let's move on to the next person."

"I-I'll go," the other boy says nervously. He's much shorter than Thermo and his stringy hair nearly covers his eyes. He's wearing flippers and snorkeling gear and carrying a bucket.

"What's your name?" I ask.

"I-I call myself Monsoon," he says.

"Oh, thank goodness," Pinball whispers. "Because if he said his name was 'Puke-in-the-Bucket Boy' I'd be bouncing out of the auditorium right now."

"Shhh!" Skunk Girl whispers back.

"Welcome, Monsoon," I say. "Well, with a name like that I'm expecting big things. Please, don't be nervous. Just show us what you can do."

"O-Okay," he says, putting the bucket on the floor. "I-I practiced but I apologize in advance if I splash you."

"Splash us?" Pinball says, grabbing his armrests. "I was just kidding. He's not really going to puke, is he?"

But before we can react, his body suddenly transforms into water and fills the bucket at his feet! I have to admit, it was impressive, but as I lean forward, waiting for the next demonstration of his power, there's nothing. Like, nothing at all for several minutes.

"Well, this is awkward," Skunk Girl whispers.

"You know," Pinball whispers. "Maybe he should call himself 'Trickle' instead of Monsoon."

"Should we check if he's okay?" Selfie asks. "He's been in that bucket a long time."

"Um, Monsoon?" I call out. "Are you okay? Do you need help?"

Suddenly, water flies up from the bucket and the next thing we know, Monsoon is back to human form!

"Sorry," he says, cleaning out his ears. "I can't hear a thing when I'm in water form. I'm so glad that worked out. Last time I missed the bucket and ended up in the toilet."

"Oh, wow," I say. "Well, thanks for that little tidbit, but can you, um, do anything else? You know, like form into a giant water torpedo or mentally control fish or anything like that?"

"Oh, no," he says. "That's it."

"I see," I say. "Well, thank you for auditioning."

"No problem," he says, picking up his bucket.

"Well, I guess that leaves me," the girl says, moving to the front of the stage. She has wild, dark hair, purple goggles, and a purple costume with the symbol of a messy spiral on her top.

"Based on the last two auditions," Pinball whispers, "I can't wait to see this one."

"I can," Skunk Girl says, covering her eyes.

"So, tell us your name and what you do," I say.

"Sure," she says. "I call myself Haywire, and my powers are, well, a little unusual."

"How so?" I ask.

Just then, a giant spotlight over the stage shoots out white, electric sparks.

"YIP!" Dog-Gone cries, jumping into my lap.

"Ow!" I yell. "Get off me you scaredy-cat!"

Then, the whole auditorium goes pitch-dark.

"Hey!" Selfie says. "Dog-Gone is biting my phone!"

"Ow!" Skunk Girl says. "Pinball, you idiot! You just elbowed me in the nose!"

"Sorry," Pinball says. "I'm stuck in my seat and can't get out!"

"Yuck!" Selfie says. "What's that smell?"

"I-I think it's me," Skunk Girl says. "For some reason, I can't control my powers!"

As I pinch my nose and try to push Dog-Gone to the floor, I wonder what happened. I mean, a second ago everything was fine, but now everything has gone completely hay... wire.

"Hold on," I say, calling up to the stage. "You're doing this, aren't you?"

"Yeah," Haywire says. "That's kind of my thing.

When I use my powers, things get out of control."

"Well, do you mind turning your powers off?" Pinball asks. "Otherwise, we'll all die from this skunk bomb."

"Very funny," Skunk Girl says.

"Sure," Haywire says. "I can stop my power but if something has already started, it'll just keep going. Like, once I was hiking with my parents in the mountains and I accidentally triggered an avalanche. Once gravity started going, I couldn't stop the rocks from falling. Fortunately, I got my parents out of the way before anyone got hurt. It was always just the three of us, but now they're gone and I'll do whatever it takes to find them."

Everyone is silent as her words hit us all.

She's right and we all feel the same way. I'll do anything to get my parents back. Even if it means breaking up Next Gen later on.

Just then, the lights come back on and I'm staring at the three eager candidates. I feel terrible because I know what it's like to be in their shoes. I mean, all I ever wanted was to join the Freedom Force. But ironically, now it's my turn to decide if they'll be joining us.

"Can you just give us a minute to discuss?" I ask.

The candidates nod and we huddle up.

"So, what do you think?" I ask the team.

"Unfortunately, it's a no for me," Selfie says.

"Hard no," Skunk Girl says.

"Big thumbs down," Pinball says.

Even Dog-Gone shakes his head 'no.'

And I can't argue. As much as I'd want to let them in, they're simply not ready. But now comes the hard part. Now I've got to deliver the bad news.

"So, here's what we think," I start.

But then—BEEP! BEEP! BEEP!

"What's that?" Selfie asks.

"My Freedom Force transmitter," I say. Following my misadventures with Krule and the Skelton Emperor, Mom made TechnocRat put a transmitter into my utility belt. She said it was to stay in closer communication, but I'm pretty sure it was for her to keep tabs on me. I press the button on the front of my belt and say, "Hello?"

"Get your squad over to the Keystone City Zoo pronto!" comes Grace's voice. "Someone is letting all of the animals loose! Kids could get hurt!"

"What?" I say. "Who would do something like that?"

"Do you think I have time to figure that out?" she barks. "That's why I called you. I'm trying to run the country here!"

CLICK!

Well, I guess that was an executive order. The zoo is filled with all sorts of dangerous animals. We're going to need help to get them back in their cages, let alone find the bad guy. Lots of help.

I look up at the hopeful faces on the stage and announce, "Congratulations, candidates. You've all made it to phase two of the audition!"

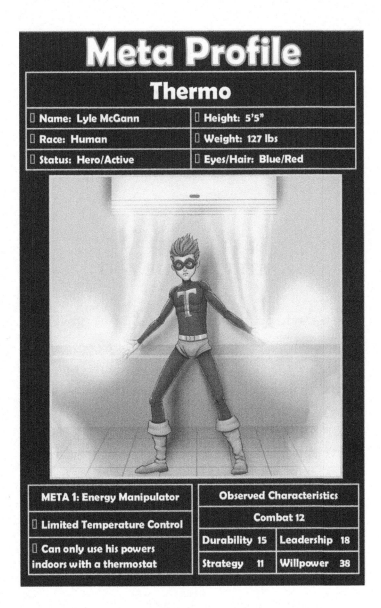

Meta Profile

Thermo

⬥ Name: Lyle McGann	⬥ Height: 5'5"
⬥ Race: Human	⬥ Weight: 127 lbs
⬥ Status: Hero/Active	⬥ Eyes/Hair: Blue/Red

META 1: Energy Manipulator	Observed Characteristics	
⬥ Limited Temperature Control	Combat 12	
⬥ Can only use his powers indoors with a thermostat	Durability 15	Leadership 18
	Strategy 11	Willpower 38

SIX

I STEW AT THE ZOO

"**W**hat were you thinking?" Selfie whispers firmly as we run through the gates of the Keystone City Zoo.

I glance over my shoulder at the three candidates trailing behind us and wonder the same thing. I mean, none of us thought these kids had what it takes to join Next Gen, but I brought them along anyway. Maybe it wasn't a great idea, but I figured we'll need all the help we can get to capture the freed animals and find the perpetrator.

The rest of the team, however, clearly doesn't agree. In fact, up until Selfie asked me that question, they've been giving me the cold shoulder. Not that I can blame them. I pretty much ignored what they had to say.

So much for being a great leader.

But I really believe that bringing these rookies along was the right decision. There's no better way for them to prove themselves. I look back again to find Haywire looking determined, Thermo looking winded, and Monsoon looking like he wants to barf into his bucket.

Okay, maybe this wasn't such a good idea after all.

Especially after I spot the lion.

"Everybody stop!" I call out, skidding to a halt.

We all slam into each other as the giant feline stares us down with his calculating pupils. He's perched on top of the ticket booth counter, licking his lips like he's found his next meal, otherwise known as us!

"Th-That's a lion!" Pinball stammers. "Um, wh-what's up, my mane man? Get it? 'Main' man?"

"You're hilarious," Skunk Girl says, rolling her eyes. "But bad jokes aren't going to get him back in his cage."

"I can try," Thermo says, assuming a karate pose.

"Um, no," I say. "Why don't you stand back."

Suddenly, the lion GROWLS and leaps gracefully to the ground with surprising speed. I can't say I've ever been this close to a lion before—or its super-sharp, boy-eating teeth! No wonder he's called the King of the Jungle! Why couldn't we have run into a koala first?

Okay, think. We're going to have to capture him, but unfortunately, lions don't have Meta powers. So, unless Dog-Gone can lure this beast over to his cage using his invisibility, we're pretty useless. But when I look around, Dog-Gone is gone! What a surprise. Not.

"Okay, move over," Selfie says, stepping forward and holding up her phone. "Look over here, Mr. Kitty Cat, and you'll start to feel very, very sleepy."

But just as she's about to push the button—

"I'll help!" Haywire says, running over to Selfie.

"No!" I call out, but it's too late because just as Selfie presses the button, a streetlamp CRASHES down in front of us and the flash from Selfie's phone reflects off the metal light fixture! I shield my eyes just in time, but when I look back up, Selfie, Skunk Girl, and Pinball are all standing stock-still with dazed expressions on their faces!

They've been hypnotized by Selfie's magic phone!

"Sorry," Haywire says. "I-I didn't know that would happen. Will they be okay?"

"Don't worry," I say, "it'll go away eventually." And speaking of 'going away,' where's the lion? I look around but he's gone. I guess the streetlamp scared him away.

"What now?" Thermo asks. "I'm ready for action."

But as I look at the three candidates I realize how *not* ready for action they actually are. I should have listened to the team. I was wrong and they were right. And my foolish decision nearly got them killed.

Suddenly, I realize how my parents must have felt when I would beg them to take me on missions when I was a Zero. And even though these kids have powers, they either can't control them or they're just not useful in a crisis. It's simply too dangerous for them to use their powers in public.

Suddenly, I flashback to my conversation with Mom and Dad. I can still hear Dad telling me what it takes to be a leader. He said a leader must assess if the team can handle the mission. And if not, the leader must protect the team from harm. Now I see how right he was, and no matter how painful it is I know what I need to do.

"Look, guys," I say, "thank you for auditioning for Next Gen, but I'm afraid we can't add any of you to the team right now."

I pause for a second to gauge their reaction. Haywire looks disappointed, Thermo looks confused, and Monsoon actually looks relieved.

"You guys have some cool powers," I continue, "but until you have better control over them and can use them in a variety of situations, it's just too dangerous for you, us, and, well, everyone else for you to operate in public. I'm really sorry but I hope you understand."

"So, wait," Thermo says, "are you saying it's over?"

"Yeah," I say. "I'm really sorry. But I'm hoping you'd be willing to do me a favor. I still have a lot of superhero stuff to do, so would you mind helping my colleagues here into one of the buildings where they'll be safe until Selfie's hypnosis power wears off?"

"Sure," Monsoon says. "Do you need my bucket?"

"Um, no," I say. "I'm good. But thanks."

"I appreciate the opportunity," Haywire says, her face looking sad. "But given my luck, I'm not surprised by your decision. Thanks for letting me try out."

"Hey, don't be down," I say. "You did your best and with more practice, you'll learn how to control your powers. Then, maybe you can try out again in the future."

"Yeah," she says, "if there even is a future. I'll help your friends get to safety, and don't worry, I'll keep my powers 'off.' But just so you know, I'm not going to stop looking for my parents. Whatever it takes, whatever I have to do, I'll find them. I'm going to be a great hero one day, even without Next Gen."

As I look into her determined eyes I'm torn. I mean, I really like her fighting spirit but I know in my gut it would be a mistake to keep her around. Her powers are just too unpredictable. Yet, she's clearly going to keep going, even without Next Gen.

"Look, I get it," I say. "I'm sure you'll be great too, but please, just practice a lot first. And be careful."

"You too," she says.

As I watch Haywire, Thermo, and Monsoon guide the others, I realize I'm all on my own. Well, all on my own except for a criminal on the premises and a billion wild animals who'd love nothing more than to eat me. Then, it dawns on me that I've got my own wild animal.

"Dog-Gone?" I call out. "Where are you, you coward? Are you really going to let a big cat scare you?"

Just then, Dog-Gone appears on the other side of the pathway. He's just sitting there, trying to look innocent but I know he feels guilty for abandoning me.

"I forgive you," I say. "Just don't disappear on me

again, got it?"

Dog-Gone barks when suddenly we hear a chorus of SCREECHING coming from our right. That sounded like a tribe of monkeys, or rather, a tribe of agitated monkeys. Maybe we'll find something there!

We run down a pathway marked PRIMATES and round the corner to find a group of capuchin monkeys swarming out of their cage. Whoever is responsible for this was just here! If I'm fast enough maybe I can catch him!

"Dog-Gone," I say. "Get these monkeys back in their cage. I'm going ahead."

As I continue, I hear Dog-Gone BARKING followed by even more SCREECHING. I don't know what's going on back there, but either he's succeeding in wrangling those monkeys or they've just tied him to the nearest tree. But I can't stop to look because I've got my own job to do.

I run past more empty cages, a lemur looting a trash can, and an emu just looking ugly before I stumble across my target standing in front of the elephant pen.

Except, he's not a 'he' at all.

Because it's... a robot?

Why is a robot letting animals out of their cages?

"Stop right there!" I order.

But as the seven-foot-tall giant turns and takes me in with its cold, red eyes, I realize I'm in big, big trouble.

"L-Let go of that gate!" I say meekly.

The robot's eyes flicker, and I get the sense that it really doesn't care what I have to say. And then I notice the strange, yellow glow coming off of its body.

What is that?

And come to think of it, why does that robot look so darn familiar? Like I've seen it somewhere before?

Suddenly, it raises an arm and its metal hand retracts into its socket only to be replaced by a gun.

Uh oh.

THOOM!

I leap into the bushes just as the laser wipes out the ground I was standing on. Okay, this bucket of bolts means business! Somehow I've got to stop it, but my powers don't work on robots. And I still can't shake why it looks so familiar? Then, its eyes flicker again.

THOOM! THOOM!

I spring from the bushes and roll behind a tree as the robot continues to track me. This isn't good. As long as I'm visible I've got no chance! So, I concentrate hard and reach out far and wide until I connect with Dog-Gone. Then, I pull in his powers and make myself invisible. At least that fleabag is good for something!

I peer around the trunk to see the robot scanning the area. Thankfully, he doesn't have infrared vision because he clearly doesn't see me. I wait for him to finish and when he turns around I step lightly into the clearing.

That's when I get another shock, because on the back of its right shoulder is a giant 'on/off' switch.

Suddenly, I realize where I've seen this guy before because that's no ordinary robot, that's a—

"Light's out, buddy!" comes a girl's voice, and the next thing I know the robot is encased in a cone of darkness!

Just then, that mysterious masked girl in black comes sailing over the elephant house on one of her shadow slides and practically lands on top of me.

"Hey!" I call out, turning visible again. "Watch where you're going!"

"You again?" she says, clearly surprised to see me. "How come you keep showing up wherever I find trouble?"

"I was going to ask you the same thing," I say.

"Really?" she says. "Well, don't worry. I've got this in hand." Then, she closes her fist and the cone of darkness solidifies and squeezes the robot, crushing it into a gazillion pieces.

"There," she says. "Crisis averted."

"Nice job," I say. "Now what are you doing here?"

"There was a gorilla loose on Main Street," she says. "And when I brought him back to the zoo I ran into other loose animals too. I figured someone was responsible for this. I just wasn't expecting it to be you."

"I'm not responsible," I say. "I'm a hero, remember? We already had this conversation."

"Yeah," she says. "I remember, I just may not believe you. Maybe you created this robot."

"It's not a robot," I say, walking over to pick up one of its pieces. But that's when I get another surprise. All of the scattered body parts have shrunken in size.

"What happened to it?" the girl asks.

"I'm not sure," I say, picking up a tiny arm. "But this 'robot' is actually called a Powerbot. It's a toy. I had a bunch of them when I was younger. You must have seen the commercials. Powerbots—weapons in disguise? They're toy robots that turn into weapons."

"Wait," she says. "So, you're saying that gigantic robot was once a toy?"

"Yeah," I say. "It's like someone made it huge and sent it to the zoo to free all the animals. But who would do that?"

"No clue," she says.

"Well, I'm going to collect all the parts and bring them to the Waystation for analysis."

"The Waystation?" she says. "Isn't that, like, the Freedom Force's headquarters?"

"Yeah," I say. "I'm a member of the Freedom Force."

"Seriously?" she says, looking at me funny. "Have they lowered their standards?"

"No," I say, staying calm. "By the way, I never caught your name."

"I'm Night Owl," she says. "I can control shadows by shifting them around and making them solid."

"That's cool," I say.

And as I look into her eyes I realize her powers and control would be perfect for Next Gen.

"Hey, listen, I know we got off on the wrong foot, well, twice, but I'm also leading a new superhero team called Next Gen. We're a bunch of Meta kids who fight for truth and justice. Funny enough, we just had a tryout for new members, and I think you would be great—"

"Whoa," she says. "Hang on there, sparky. I'm not much of a joiner. I prefer working alone."

"Okay," I say, taken aback by her strong reaction. "I get it, but given the current state of the world maybe you'd reconsider and—"

"Look, it's been fun saving you—again—but I've really got to go," she says, generating another shadow slide. "So, while you and your friends pretend to play superhero, I'm going to round up the rest of these animals. Oh, and one last thing before I go, I'm warning you, I've got my eyes on you."

And before I can respond, she takes off.

Well, that didn't go well. And as I watch her disappear over the treetops, I realize another challenge has been added to my list. I need to prove to her that I'm not a villain.

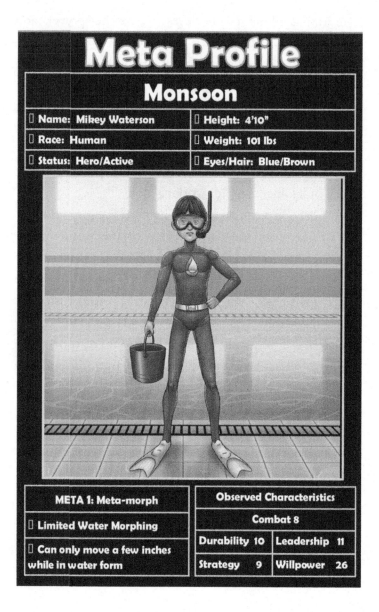

Meta Profile

Monsoon

Name: Mikey Waterson	Height: 4'10"
Race: Human	Weight: 101 lbs
Status: Hero/Active	Eyes/Hair: Blue/Brown

META 1: Meta-morph	Observed Characteristics	
Limited Water Morphing	Combat 8	
Can only move a few inches while in water form	Durability 10	Leadership 11
	Strategy 9	Willpower 26

SEVEN

I GET A CLUE

Time is clearly of the essence.

I mean, not only are all of the grown-ups missing, but Grace will turn fifteen in just a few days. So, it's not like there's time to sit around twiddling my thumbs. As Grace said, this is a time for swift action, which is why I did something that would normally get me in heaps of trouble.

I brought Next Gen up to the Waystation.

You see, we have a sacred rule that no outsiders can visit the Waystation. And the rule exists for good reason because there are all sorts of top-secret and dangerous things up here. But right now, I have to throw rules out the window. Besides, it's not like there's anyone around to argue with me.

I put the team in the Medi-wing so they could recover from Selfie's hypnosis power. Then, I left Dog-Gone behind to keep an eye on them, which was probably a mistake since he has the attention span of a fruit fly. But I can't worry about that now because I need to analyze that Powerbot toy to figure out how it came alive.

Luckily, I managed to collect all of its parts except for a leg, and I'm hoping that strange, yellow energy coming from its body will provide the clue I need. But as I navigate through the halls I can't stop thinking about what Night Owl said. She has some nerve accusing me of being responsible for this. She doesn't know me at all.

Yet, I still feel bad for wanting space from my parents. But I'm sure I'm not the only kid who ever wanted that. I mean, there's no way this could be my fault. Could it?

I hang a left and then a right and find myself standing in front of a sliding double door with a sign that reads: TECHNOCRAT'S LABORATORY. DANGER. DO NOT ENTER. ELLIOTT, THAT MEANS YOU!

Well, I have to admit, that rat has quite the sense of humor. But funny guy or not, I need to get inside his lab to properly analyze these toy parts.

The problem is, he told me he changed his passcode when he built the Waystation 2.0. I stare at the keypad and do some deep thinking. There are nine entry fields so I need a code with nine letters. There's no way he would use CAMEMBERT again, would he? I mean, he knows I figured it out last time.

So, what else has nine letters? I try hard to get inside the mind of a rat, but it's not easy. What does he love? Hmm, maybe? I punch C-O-M-P-U-T-E-R-S into the keypad and the console spits back:

ERROR: TWO ATTEMPTS REMAINING.

Great. Why does this seem like déjà vu all over again? For some reason, I can't think of anything else and that's when I realize he's probably playing mind games with me. Knowing him, I bet he never changed his password at all! That would be just like him to use reverse psychology on me. Well, I'm no fool.

I type in C-A-M-E-M-B-E-R-T and wait for the doors to slide open, but instead, I get:

ERROR: ONE ATTEMPT REMAINING.

Aaaaaaah!

He got me! I'm such a fool! And now I've wasted an attempt! I need to get inside so I can analyze these parts. I just need the freaking passcode! In my mind's eye, I can just picture TechnocRat standing there all smug with his little arms crossed and saying, "Holy guacamole, you *are* clueless aren't you?" And I would say…

Wait a minute! Could it be?

But if I screw this up, I'll kiss my chance of getting inside goodbye. But it's my only shot, so I take a deep breath and type: G-U-A-C-A-M-O-L-E.

Suddenly, the console turns green and the doors slide

open! I did it! I'm in!

As soon as I step inside I realize cracking the code was probably the easy part because TechnocRat's refurbished lab is twice the size of his previous one, which only means it's twice as messy. Clutter is piled high as far as my eyes can see—on the floor, on the desks, and even climbing the walls! This is going to be tough because I'm looking for one piece of equipment in particular.

The Meta Spectrometer.

The Meta Spectrometer is a device TechnocRat invented to identify hard to read Meta powers—including my own. When my powers finally showed up, there was no way to figure out what they actually were. In fact, at the time there wasn't even a classification for Meta Manipulation! But by using the Meta Spectrometer, Technocrat was able to analyze my unique Meta signature to determine that my powers were unlike anyone else's on the planet, except for Meta-Taker.

So, I figure if I feed these toy parts into the Meta Spectrometer then maybe it can identify what that weird yellow energy was. The problem is, I need to find the device first. Now where could it be?

I dig through papers, instruments, and random thingamajigs before I finally find what I'm looking for beneath a stack of blueprints. The Meta Spectrometer looks exactly how I remember it, which is sort of like a mini slot machine. You can either set the Meta Spectrometer on 'scan' or put an object directly inside.

So, I dust it off and place the toy parts into the compartment.

Then, I pull the lever.

A tiny hourglass icon appears on the monitor along with the words: *CURRENTLY ANALYZING. THIS MAY TAKE SEVERAL MINUTES SO NOW IS A GOOD TIME TO GET SOME CHEESE.*

Boy, that rat never misses an opportunity for cheese.

Well, there's no use hanging around while the Meta Spectrometer is doing its thing, so I decide to head back to the Medi-wing to check on the others. As my footsteps echo through the halls I realize how strange it feels to be up here without the Freedom Force. I used to be here alone all the time when I didn't have powers, but now we're usually together. And every time I turn a corner I expect to run into Blue Bolt or Shadow Hawk or my parents.

But they're not here.

Suddenly, I feel tears welling up in my eyes. I mean, so much has happened since they disappeared that I haven't had time for it to sink in. I want to stay hopeful, but I don't know where they are or even if they're still alive. I shudder at the thought but as much as I don't want to think it, I can't rule it out. I guess deep down I need to prepare myself for anything.

As I reach the Medi-wing I pause, wipe my eyes, and go through the door. I need to be strong for the team. If I break down they might lose hope. After all, we're the ones who need to find out what happened. Luckily, they're all sitting up and looking much more like themselves. "How do you feel?" I ask.

"Fine," Selfie says, rubbing her cheeks, "embarrassed but fine."

"It's not your fault," I say. "You got caught in Haywire's bad luck. It could've happened to any of us."

"That girl is a walking disaster," Skunk Girl says. "Her costume should be a big, yellow warning sign."

"You've got that right," Pinball says. "The next time I see her coming I'm going the other way."

"Hey, take it easy on her," I say. "She meant well. She's just inexperienced, that's all."

"Speaking of inexperienced," comes a familiar voice from behind me, "what are these kids doing here? You know we're not allowed to bring outsiders to the Waystation."

I turn to find Grace scowling in the doorway.

"They're not 'outsiders,' they're my team and... forget it," I say. "The real question is what are *you* doing here? I thought you were busy running the country?"

"I am," she says, "but I need to broadcast a State of the Union Address so I thought I'd do it from here. But since your 'team' is around they can help."

"A State of the Union?" Pinball says. "What's that?"

"It's when the president addresses the nation, dumbo," Skunk Girl says.

"Exactly," Grace says. "So, get your rumps in gear,

and let's go."

"Is she always this bossy?" Selfie asks.

"Yep," I answer. "But it's always worse when we're out of jelly doughnuts."

We follow Grace to the Media Room, which is another one of the snazzy new additions TechnocRat added to the Waystation 2.0. The Media Room is basically a studio space where we can film communications or conduct interviews with the media back on Earth. Grace stands behind the podium in front of the American flag and whips out her compact mirror.

"Wow," Pinball says, looking around. "This headquarters sure beats the Hangout. By like, a lot."

"Epic Zero," Grace barks while picking food out of her teeth, "you manage the camera. Selfie, you make sure he stays on my good side—slightly left at a fifteen-degree angle. Skunk Lass, you make sure my lighting is perfect. I don't want shadows under my eyes."

"It's 'Girl'," Skunk Girl says. "Skunk 'Girl.'"

"And what about me, Madame President?" Pinball asks. "What can I do?"

"You?" Grace says, looking him up and down. "You keep your eye on the dog and make sure he doesn't steal the limelight. This is my moment."

"Yes, Ma'am," Pinball says with a salute, and then steps in front of Dog-Gone who looks none too happy about it. "You sit. I've got both eyes on you."

"Great, let's get my speech filmed first, and then

we'll post it to all the social media channels," Grace says, snapping her compact mirror closed. "Hit the lights, Skunk Gal, it's showtime!"

I hear Skunk Girl groan as she flicks on the lights.

"Check the angle," Grace says, as I aim the camera.

"Relax, I've got it," I tell Selfie. "Okay, I'm hitting the record button in three, two, one…"

Grace stands up straight, flashes a big smile, and says with great gusto, "Greetings, citizens of Earth! I—"

"Whoa!" I say, stopping the camera. "Seriously? Greetings, citizens of Earth? What are you, an alien conqueror? And you're coming on way too strong. You need to be cool and collected. People are already panicking out there."

"Okay, okay," Grace says, looking annoyed. "I'll start over. And make sure to check the camera angle."

"I'm good," I say. "And three, two, one…"

"Good evening, fellow Americans," Grace says, sounding more calm and deliberate. "As you already know, I'm Glory Girl of the Freedom Force. This morning we woke up to a terrible tragedy that has left our nation reeling. The grown-ups in our world, including those aged fifteen and older, have vanished without a trace. At the moment we don't know who is behind this or what their motivations might be, but I can assure you we are on the case. However, due to the absence of anyone in authority, we are now experiencing a gap in leadership for our country."

I have to admit, she's actually doing a good job.

"Therefore," she continues, putting a hand over her heart, "despite my initial reservations, I simply could not ignore the thousands of text messages, emails, and personal pleas begging me to step into a leadership role. So, after a lot of soul searching, I have selflessly and humbly decided to assume the role of President of the United States to help our nation get back on our feet."

Um, what? That's not how it happened. Okay, now she's going a little off the rails.

"To that end," she carries on, "I have laid out a five-point plan to help our nation return to prosperity which I will share with you now. Point number one, from this day forward, all Metas will respectfully treat me as Commander and Chief and follow my orders without question. Point number two—"

"Okay, cut!" I say, turning off the camera.

"What are you doing?" Grace asks. "I have four more points to outline."

"The only point you've outlined is the one on your head," I say. "You're getting power-hungry."

"I am not!" Grace objects.

"Is she getting power-hungry?" I ask, turning to Pinball.

"Well, maybe just an eensy-weensy bit power-hungry," he says, closing his thumb and forefinger.

"See?" I say. "And he's the only one here who actually voted for you."

"Turn that camera back on!" Grace orders. "I'm your president! You have to listen to me!"

"No, I don't," I say. "You elected yourself!"

"Well, this is fun," Skunk Girl says.

"ANALYSIS COMPLETE," comes a mechanical voice over the intercom system.

"Um, what was that?" Selfie asks.

"The Meta Spectrometer!" I say, booking out of the Media Room. With all of Grace's ridiculousness, I almost forgot about it! Thank goodness TechnocRat had it hooked up to the intercom system.

"Come back!" Grace demands, but I'm already gone.

And I guess the team has had enough of her too because they're right behind me, including Pinball.

I lead the team to TechnocRat's lab and race over to the Meta Spectrometer.

"Um, what are we doing here?" Pinball asks, looking at all the mess. "Because this place doesn't seem very hygienic."

"Hang on," I say. "I put the toy parts into this device to see if we could identify its Meta classification."

Then, I look at the console which reads: PRESS BUTTON FOR RESULTS. Yes! Here we go. I push the button and my jaw drops. Because the console reads:

META CLASS: MAGIC.

META SUB-TYPE: BLACK MAGIC.

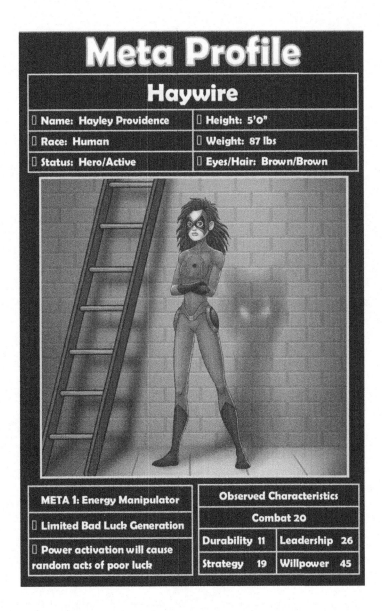

Meta Profile

Haywire

⬜ Name: Hayley Providence	⬜ Height: 5'0"
⬜ Race: Human	⬜ Weight: 87 lbs
⬜ Status: Hero/Active	⬜ Eyes/Hair: Brown/Brown

META 1: Energy Manipulator	Observed Characteristics	
⬜ Limited Bad Luck Generation	Combat 20	
⬜ Power activation will cause random acts of poor luck	Durability 11	Leadership 26
	Strategy 19	Willpower 45

EIGHT

I DON'T WANT TO BELIEVE IN MAGIC

I have to say, I'm kind of shocked right now.

When I fed the toy parts into the Meta Spectrometer to analyze the strange, yellow energy they were emitting, it never crossed my mind that it would come back as Black Magic. I mean, I've never faced a Meta who used Black Magic before.

"Um, I'm guessing that's not good," Pinball says.

"Nope," I say, "probably not."

"Sorry for being dense here," Skunk Girl says, "but what exactly is Black Magic anyway?"

"Well," I say, trying to think of how best to answer her question, "Magic is one of the nine major classifications of Meta powers. Metas who use Magic, like Master Mime, and even Selfie here, typically channel their powers through an enchanted object. For example, Selfie's power comes from her phone which she uses for good. Black Magic works the same way, but the power inside the enchanted object typically comes from a dark source, like a demon, a departed soul, or a dark realm. You know, something like that."

"Well, that sounds ominous," Skunk Girl says.

"So, if that toy was giving off Black Magic," Selfie says, "do you think the toy itself was the enchanted object?"

That's another good question. But as I think about it, Night Owl shattered that Powerbot with ease. Could an enchanted object really break that easily? I mean, Master Mime's amulet is super solid, and Selfie's phone is way more durable than a normal phone.

"No," I say. "I don't think so. I think somebody else used their power on the toy robot and that's what the Meta Spectrometer picked up."

"The question is *who*?" Pinball asks.

Yep, that is the big question.

Who? Who? Who?

"Hold on!" I blurt out as a lightbulb goes on in my brain. Sometimes I'm such a dufus. "We *can* find out who did it right here. All we have to do is feed the reading from the Meta Spectrometer directly into the Meta Monitor and see if we get a Meta Profile match."

"Um, is it just me or is he speaking Meta gibberish?" Skunk Girl asks.

"Just follow me," I say, pressing a button on the Meta Spectrometer to extract the reading onto a printout.

As soon as it spits out the paper, I grab it and head for the exit. I lead the team back through the Waystation and up the twenty-three steps to the Monitor Room 2.0. TechnocRat did a great job rebuilding the Monitor Room with plenty of enhancements, including a soda machine. But the best feature of all is the improved Meta Monitor. This version is far more sensitive than the last one, so it should be able to pick up even the slightest indication of a power signature. I hop into the command chair.

"This headquarters is incredible," Pinball says, admiring the soda machine. "I bet there's even a swimming pool."

"There is," I say, typing into the keyboard. "But I can't give you a tour right now. Okay, fingers crossed."

Then, I insert the printout from the Meta Spectrometer into the Meta Monitor. As the Meta Monitor ingests the paper, I can barely contain my excitement. I mean, this could be the break we've been looking for. This could tell us who is responsible for the grown-ups disappearing.

Just then, another spinning hourglass flashes on the screen with the familiar words: *CURRENTLY ANALYZING. THIS MAY TAKE SEVERAL MINUTES SO NOW IS A GOOD TIME TO GET SOME CHEESE.*

Gotta love that rat. At least he's consistent.

"I'd love some cheese right now," Pinball says, patting his stomach. "And crackers. I'd love some crackers too."

"Can't you stop thinking about your stomach for a minute?" Skunk Girl says. "This is serious."

"I'm serious too," Pinball says. "Seriously hungry."

Suddenly, the screen flashes green and the words on the monitor read: META PROFILE IDENTIFIED.

"Yes!" I say, pumping my fist. "We're about to get our answer."

Just then, a Meta profile kicks up. It reads:

- *Beezle*
- *Race: Djinn*
- *Status: Villain/Inactive*
- *Height: Unknown*
- *Weight: Unknown*
- *Eye Color: Yellow*
- *Hair Color: Bald*
- *Meta Class: Magic*
- *Meta Level: Meta 2*
- *Considerable Wish Fulfillment Power*
- *Considerable Mind-Warping Power*
- *Considerable Shapeshifting Power*
- *Beezle is only able to use his powers if he has a human guide to steer it.*
- *Known Origin: Beezle is one of three brothers known as the Djinn Three. The other brothers of the Djinn Three*

are Rasp and Terrog. The Djinn Three are believed to be thousands of years old and have plagued mankind for centuries. Each of the Djinn Three is bound to one of three mystical rings known as the Rings of Suffering and possess varying levels of observed Meta powers. Rasp (Meta 1) is bound to the bronze ring, Beezle (Meta 2) is bound to the silver ring, and Terrog (Meta 3) is bound to the gold ring. Once a ring is placed on the finger, the Djinn Three are freed from their ring to grant their host three wishes. The Djinn Three also possess varying levels of mind-warping power that can influence their host's desires. The only way to stop the Djinn Three is to trap them back inside their respective ring. It is unknown who created the Rings of Suffering. Currently, all three rings are safely in the possession of the Freedom Force.

I swallow hard and read that last part again:

Currently, all three rings are safely in the possession of the Freedom Force.

I check the date of the last update which was over two years ago. Suddenly, I feel like I'm gonna puke.

"Well, that Beezle guy sounds like the life of the party," Skunk Girl says.

"Epic Zero, are you okay?" Selfie asks. "You look like you've seen a ghost."

"I… I…," I stammer, but the words just don't come out. I mean, it says all three Rings of Suffering are safely in the possession of the Freedom Force, but from what I remember, only one ring was in the Trophy Room.

Which means…

I take off.

"Epic Zero?" Selfie calls out. "Wait, where are you going?"

But by the time she finishes I'm already halfway down the stairs, hoping my mind was just playing tricks on me. I hear shouting and footsteps behind me and look back to see Dog-Gone and the others on my tail, but I can't stop. I need to check for myself.

Seconds later, I'm inside the Trophy Room. I hang a left at the giant brain and make my way over to the display case in question: The Three Rings of Suffering.

But as I look inside I feel like someone punched me in the gut because I was right. There's only one ring here and it's the bronze one which supposedly holds Rasp. That means the other two rings are missing—and I'm pretty sure I know what happened to them!

All three rings must have been on the Waystation 1.0 before the Meta-Busters blew it up trying to murder me. After that, the Freedom Force must have only recovered one of the rings. So, the silver one containing Beezle must have been blown to Earth! And who knows where the gold one might be!

"Epic Zero?" Selfie says, catching up to us. "Are you okay? Why did you run off like that?"

"Well, that's my exercise for the day," Pinball says, breathing heavily. "That was a full-on sprint."

"Wait, is that one of the rings?" Skunk Girl asks,

looking inside the display case. "That's the bronze one! So, there must be a djinn in there!"

"Did you say dinner is in there?" Pinball asks. "That's great because I'm starving."

"Not dinner, you dufus, a djinn," Skunk Girl says. "A djinn is like a genie, but an evil one."

"In that case," Pinball says, "I'll order room service."

"So, is that for real?" Selfie asks, looking at the ring. "But I thought the Freedom Force had all three. What happened to the other two?"

I'm about to answer but stop myself. I mean, is there really any reason to tell them my theory on what happened to the other rings? After all, I feel bad enough already. Especially because I know it's somehow tied to the toy robot and the grown-ups disappearing.

Wait, that's it!

"Epic?" Selfie says. "What's wrong?"

"Nothing," I say. "In fact, everything is starting to make sense. Because if that djinn named Beezle was responsible for turning that toy into a giant, then that means it's on Earth. Which means we may be able to pinpoint its location. Come on!"

"Seriously?" Pinball says. "We're running again?"

I lead the team back the way we came and hustle up the steps to the Monitor Room. Then, I get to work.

"What are you doing?" Skunk Girl asks.

"Plugging in Beezle's Meta signature," I answer. "The Meta Monitor is programmed to identify Meta powers. Every power has a unique signature, and now that we've matched that signature to Beezle, it's only a matter of time before the Meta Monitor finds him."

"That's cool," Pinball says, leaning against a console, "as long as we can stop rushing back and forth. You know, they say too much exercise isn't healthy. I think I heard a guy who played a doctor on TV mention it once."

"Alert! Alert! Alert!" the Meta Monitor blares. "Meta 2 disturbance. Repeat: Meta 2 disturbance. Power signature identified as Beezle. Alert! Alert! Alert! Meta 2 disturbance. Power signature identified as Beezle."

"Bingo!" I say. "We've got him!"

"Where is he?" Selfie asks.

Just then, the location pops up on the monitor and my heart starts racing because it reads:

META SIGNATURE IDENTIFIED.

LOCATION: LOCKDOWN META-MAXIMUM FEDERAL PENITENTIARY.

Meta Profile
Three Rings of Suffering

THREE RINGS OF SUFFERING
Gold Ring: Terrog (Meta 3) - click link for Meta Profile
Silver Ring: Beezle (Meta 2) - click link for Meta Profile
Bronze Ring: Rasp (Meta 1) - click link for Meta Profile

NINE

I PLAY LET'S MAKE A DEAL

This is the last place I expected to be right now.

I mean, my history with Lockdown isn't exactly a good one. And as I think back to all of my misadventures with this place, nothing sticks out more than the death of my friend K'ami. I still have nightmares about that horrific moment in the courtyard—that moment when K'ami died in my arms.

But no matter how painful that memory is, I have to soldier on. There's just too much at stake and too many people counting on me to back out now. So, I need to focus on the task at hand, which is finding Beezle.

I touch down the Freedom Flyer inside the gates. Under normal circumstances, I wouldn't be able to get close to the facility without being barraged by security.

But clearly, these aren't normal circumstances. And once we're on the ground, there's nothing between us and the front door.

"Well, this place is creepy," Pinball says. "Maybe I'll wait inside the Freedom Flyer until you're done."

Wow, and I thought Dog-Gone was chicken. Yet, Pinball may have the right idea because this could be dangerous. I mean, I didn't really want to bring the team with me, but I couldn't just leave them on the Waystation.

Thankfully, I brought some extra muscle.

"Sorry," Grace says, cracking her knuckles, "but if you want to be a real superhero then you'll need to put your big boy pants on. This prison is massive and we need all hands on deck."

"Okay, okay," Pinball says, exiting the Freedom Flyer with the rest of us, "but I don't have a good feeling about this."

"Relax," Skunk Girl says. "The prison should be empty. Logically speaking, if all the grown-ups are gone then the prisoners should be gone too, right?"

"Let's hope so, Skunkie," Grace says.

I hear Skunk Girl mutter under her breath.

Skunk Girl's logic makes sense except for one small crack in her theory. If everyone is gone, then how did the Meta Monitor pick up Beezle's signature inside of Lockdown? Needless to say, I'm feeling far less 'relaxed' about this mission than she is.

We reach the entrance and when I grab the handle

and push, the front door swings open with ease. Well, that was suspiciously unlocked. I look back at Grace who nods and I step inside. The entryway looks the same as I remember, dark and narrow with small sconces lining the walls. And the air conditioning system is still too loud and pumping out way too much cold air.

"W-Well, this is j-just l-lovely," Pinball says, his teeth chattering.

But as we move past the unmanned control room and veer left, I'm surprised to find two doors instead of one. Well, this is different. I remember Dad saying he had to restructure the facility given the increase in Meta prisoners, but I didn't realize he split the actual prison into two wings.

A sign over the first door reads: *Meta Wing A: Energy Manipulators, Flyers, Magicians, Meta-Manipulators, Meta-morphs: Official Access Only.* The sign over the second door reads: *Meta Wing B: Psychics, Super-Intellects, Super-Speedsters, Super-Strength, Official Access Only.*

Well, as Grace said, this facility is massive and Beezle could be anywhere. And since we need to cover as much ground as quickly as possible there's only one conclusion.

"We should split up," I suggest.

"Great idea," Grace says. "You boys take Wing A and us girls will take Wing B."

"Deal," I say. "C'mon, Dog-Gone and Pinball."

"Hang on," Pinball says. "I want to go with Glory Girl. I think we'd make great partners!"

"Sorry," Grace says. "Girls rule, boys drool. Later."

As the girls head off, Pinball looks dejected, but I'm hoping he'll get over it. After all, Wing A is exactly where I want to be because it's the wing holding the Magicians. And since Beezle uses Magic maybe we'll find something.

I open the door and step inside.

"Do you think Glory Girl goes for younger men?" Pinball asks. "Because she's amazing."

"Dude, really?" I whisper. "We're trying to find an evil genie in a prison right now, so please focus."

"Right," he whispers.

Sometimes I wish I could forget things as easily as Pinball, but unfortunately, that's not going to happen. As we make our way through the Energy Manipulator cell block I see familiar names on the doors, like Taser, Heatwave, Magneton, and the Atomic Rage. But when I look through the cell windows there's no one inside.

And it's the same as we pass by the Flyers. Notorious villains like Atmo-Spear, Bicyclone, and Fly-Guy are all missing in action. I guess Skunk Girl was right. Since the prisoners were all grown-ups they disappeared too. So, did the Meta Monitor make a mistake? Maybe there's no one here but us.

But even if that's true, there's still one area I need to check out. We enter the Magician cell block when Dog-Gone suddenly bares his teeth and lets out a low growl.

"What's up with him?" Pinball whispers. "He's freaking me out."

"I don't know," I whisper back. "Dog-Gone, what is it? Do you smell something?"

But Dog-Gone doesn't answer.

In fact, he doesn't move at all!

"Dog-Gone, are you okay?" I ask, but when I touch his head he doesn't react. That's when I realize he's not blinking! It's like he's frozen solid even though he's not cold to the touch! "Pinball, quick—," I start, but when I turn around Pinball is frozen too!

What's going on?

Suddenly, a chill runs down my spine and I spin around. Did something just move? "Come out and face me, Beezle!" I call out, my voice cracking nervously as it echoes through the cell block.

But there's no response.

My eyes dart all over the place when I spot something I didn't see before. One of the cell doors in the Magician section is open. That's strange because none of the doors were open before. I blink hard and look again but I wasn't imagining things.

The door is still open.

Okay, this is weird. Now what? Do I check it out myself or go find Grace? But I can't just leave Dog-Gone and Pinball here like this. So, I guess I have my answer.

It's time to put my own big boy pants on.

But as I tiptoe over to the door I realize Beezle's Meta profile didn't say anything about him being able to freeze people like statues. So, how did that happen? You know, maybe this isn't such a good idea.

But when I try to stop myself, I can't! In fact, despite my best efforts, my feet just keep moving forward. It's like I'm trapped in my own body and I can't get out!

As I approach the cell, I realize the nameplate on the door is blank. Okay, that's unusual because I know every cell is specifically designed to resist the powers of its inhabitant. I try to stop, to slow myself down, but I can't. I'm being pulled in against my will!

And then I'm inside.

But the cell is no longer a cell, but a cave, complete with rock walls and a musty smell. I look around totally confused. I mean, how did that happen?

"Welcome, Epic Zero," comes a smooth, male voice.

Huh? But when I look back to the center of the room there's a man cloaked in shadows sitting at a table. Um, what's going on here? He wasn't there a second ago, and neither were the table and chairs.

"Please, join me," he says, beckoning me closer.

My feet start doing their own thing again, and as I get closer the shadows fall away from his face and I do a double-take, because he has long, dark hair, yellow eyes, and purple skin!

Okay, this clearly isn't Beezle, so I flip through all of the Meta profiles I can remember but come up empty. I don't know who this guy is, but I notice he's not wearing Beezle's silver ring.

"It's an honor to finally meet the all-powerful Epic

Zero," he says. His tone is strangely warm, like how honey would sound if it could talk. "Or would you rather be called Elliott Harkness?" Then, he offers me the chair on the other side of the table. "Please, have a seat."

But before I can object my body starts moving and plops me in the seat across from him.

"Yes, and now that you're here I can sense I was right," he says, closing his eyes and inhaling deeply. "Your aura is strong. Unusually strong."

"H-How do you know my name?" I stammer.

"Oh, I know lots of things," he says, putting his long fingers into a steeple and tapping the tips together. "You see, knowing things is my business, and I know all about you. I know what you eat for breakfast, I know who your parents are, and I even know what you're doing here. You're looking for clues like this, aren't you?"

Then, an object appears on the table and I gasp.

"That's the toy leg!" I exclaim. "That's the one piece I couldn't find at the zoo. H-How did you get it?"

"It's not important," he says, waving a hand dismissively. "But it helped get you here."

Get me here? What's he talking about? Was this a trap? "Where's Beezle?" I demand.

"Not here," the man says. "But I can help you find him if you'd like?"

"Wh-Who are you?" I ask.

"I'm known by many names," the man says. "But I prefer my true name, Tormentus."

Tormentus?

I don't know any Metas by that name.

"What do you want?" I ask.

"To be business partners," Tormentus says, his left eyebrow rising. "Maybe even friends. I suppose it depends on the bargain we strike."

"The bargain we strike?" I repeat. "What are you talking about?" And then I realize something. This guy is the only adult left on the entire freaking planet. But why? Unless...

"You look like you have a question," he says.

"A-Are you responsible for what happened to the grown-ups?" I ask. "What did you do to them? Where did you send them?"

"Slow down," Tormentus says, sitting back in his chair. "I knew you had questions, but I didn't expect so many at once."

"What did you do to the grown-ups?" I yell.

"*I* didn't do anything," Tormentus says. "But as I said, knowing things is my business, and that particular answer comes at a price."

"What are you even talking about?" I say, totally confused. "Why am I here?"

"It's actually quite simple," he says, picking up the toy leg. "You see, I'm willing to offer you a deal for the knowledge you seek. I'll tell you how to get your precious grown-ups back in exchange for something relatively small in comparison. Something rather meaningless in the grand scheme of things."

"Um, okay," I say. "And what's that?"

"Your soul," Tormentus says matter-of-factly.

"Excuse me?" I say.

"It's a no-brainer," Tormentus says. "I'll tell you how to get your loved ones and all of the others back, and in exchange, you'll give me your soul when you die. Think about it, you'll restore the lives of billions, and save your sister. Why, you'll be the greatest hero who ever lived. All for something you won't even need when your time comes. What do you say?"

I have to admit, what he's saying makes sense. I mean, if that's all it takes to bring the grown-ups back, then why wouldn't I do it? I'd get my parents back and keep Grace around. She'd owe me big time. Besides, do I really need my soul when I'm gone anyway?

"Just say 'yes,'" Tormentus says, "and I'll grant you your heart's desire. Imagine the fame you'll gain. Imagine the adulation. You'd be the greatest hero of all time."

The greatest hero of all time?

I'd like that. But wait a second. I don't care about fame and adulation—whatever that means. What's happening here? I feel like he's inside my head. Like he's brainwashing me. But that's not gonna happen. I'm not giving my soul to this nutjob!

"Sorry," I say, digging down and pushing my negation powers out, "but the answer is no! This soul can't be bought!"

Suddenly, the table and chairs disappear and I land hard on my rump. And when I look up, Tormentus is standing over me, shaking his head from side to side.

"Foolish child," he says. "You just turned down the deal of a lifetime. But don't sweat it, because someone else took me up on my generous offer. And while her soul may not be as powerful as yours, it's not as naïve. But have no fear, Elliott Harkness, I'm sure you'll get another bite at the apple real soon. And who knows? You might change your mind when your own life is on the line."

And then he snaps his fingers and he's gone!

Just then, something rattles by my feet and I pick it up. It's the toy leg! But as I squeeze it tight Tormentus' words sink in.

He said someone else took him up on his offer.

Who could that be?

But then, I look at the toy leg in my hand and have my answer.

Meta Profile

Rasp

Name: Rasp	Height: Variable
Race: Djinn	Weight: Variable
Status: Villain/Inactive	Eyes/Hair: Gray/Bald

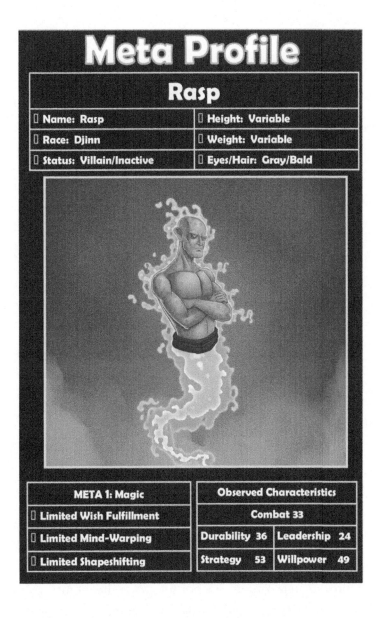

META 1: Magic	Observed Characteristics	
Limited Wish Fulfillment	Combat 33	
Limited Mind-Warping	Durability 36	Leadership 24
Limited Shapeshifting	Strategy 53	Willpower 49

TEN

I FIND OUT HOO DID IT

Thankfully, Dog-Gone and Pinball are back to normal.

Well, I guess they were never really 'normal' to begin with so let's just say they're back to their usual annoying selves. But what's strange is that Pinball doesn't even remember being frozen. And when we caught up with Grace, Selfie, and Skunk Girl they said they didn't see another soul in their entire wing.

Another soul.

What an interesting choice of words.

So, that makes me the only one who actually saw Tormentus. Lucky me. I still don't know why he wanted my soul but he certainly was pushy about getting it. Unfortunately for him, it's not for sale at the moment.

Yet, I do feel kind of guilty for not taking him up on

his deal. But the thing is, I don't know if that's how I really feel or if he's somehow still influencing my thinking. But even if I took his offer and got my parents back, I know they wouldn't approve of what I had to do to get it done. Besides, the fact that Tormentus revealed it was even possible to get them back tells me it can still be done.

I just need to figure out how.

The good news is that he left some pretty big clues. He said someone else agreed to his bargain already, and that someone is a 'she' whose soul is less naïve than mine. Funny, I don't think anyone has insulted my soul before but I guess there's a first time for everything. But while that was interesting, it's the toy leg he left behind that'll help me crack this case wide open.

After recapping my run-in with Tormentus, we race to the Freedom Flyer to confirm my suspicions. And I'm pretty sure I'm right because there was only one other person at the zoo who helped me fight that giant Powerbot. And that person also happens to be a girl. She's the only one who could have delivered that toy leg to Tormentus. So, I think I know exactly who took him up on his offer.

Night Owl.

"Never heard of her," Grace says, looking over my shoulder as I type into the dashboard console.

"I hadn't either," I say. "But now I've run into her twice and she actually thinks I'm responsible for this mess. Can you believe it?"

"No," Grace says. "Unless, of course, you are?"

"What?" I say, turning to look her dead in the eyes. "Are you kidding me? I'm not!"

"Okay, relax," Grace says. "I'm just double-checking. I mean, even you have to admit that strange stuff always happens to you. Stuff that never happens to, like, ninety-nine percent of other Meta heroes. Bad luck follows you around like a black cloud."

"Yeah," I say fuming, "but not this time."

Even though I'm annoyed with her I get what she's saying. It's true I've had some weird things happen to me, but they mostly weren't my fault. And in this case, Night Owl is the missing link. That's why I'm having the Meta Monitor triangulate her Meta signatures over the last few days. Then we'll be able to pinpoint her location.

"So, are you really sure this Night Owl kid knows what's going on?" Grace asks.

"Positive," I say. "I'm sure she's the one who made a deal with Tormentus, so you can stop watching me like a hawk."

"Are they fighting again?" I hear Skunk Girl whisper from the back of the Freedom Flyer.

"Like cats and dogs," Pinball whispers back.

"Alert! Alert! Alert!" the Meta Monitor blares. "Meta 2 disturbance. Repeat: Meta 2 disturbance. Power signature identified as Night Owl. Alert! Alert! Alert! Meta 2 disturbance. Power signature identified as Night Owl."

"Bingo!" I say. "Now we just need the location."

Then, the cursor spits out:

META SIGNATURE IDENTIFIED.

LOCATION: 224 SHADOW LAKE LANE, KEYSTONE CITY USA.

"That's it!" I say. "We've got her! And based on the map I think that's her home address."

"Okay," Selfie says. "So, now what?"

"Now?" I say. "Now we make a house call."

***

"I didn't know superheroes made house calls," Pinball says as we crowd onto the doorstep of 224 Shadow Lake Lane.

"You wouldn't believe some of the things we do," I say. But as I reach to press the doorbell I hesitate. I mean, the house is a lovely blue-and-white colonial in a nice family neighborhood with neatly trimmed hedges and gnome statues in the garden. There's nothing here that screams "sketchy character on the premises."

Maybe I've got this all wrong.

"Can you just ring the doorbell so we can get this over with already?" Grace asks from the back.

"Hold on," Skunk Girl says from behind me. "If this girl is home, do you really think she's gonna open the door for five costumed kids and a masked dog? I say we break the door down and take her by surprise."

"Break the door down?" Pinball says. "But that'll be impossible to repair. I mean, there aren't any handymen around."

"Well, then I'll smoke her out," Skunk Girl offers, wiggling her fingers. "I'll stink up the whole joint and she'll come running."

"Can someone please ring the stupid doorbell?" Grace barks. "This is getting ridiculous."

Ugh! With all of this commotion, I can't think straight. Note to self: next time we agree on the plan before deboarding the Freedom Flyer. "Can we all just calm—"

DING-DONG!

"—down?"

Huh? Who rang the doorbell?

Then, I turn to see Dog-Gone's nose pressed against the button.

"Thank you!" Grace says. "At least one of you idiots has some sense. I just didn't think it'd be the dog."

Everyone quiets down as we wait for Night Owl to answer the door, but she doesn't come.

"Told you she wouldn't open it," Skunk Girl huffs.

"What now, genius?" Grace asks.

Now there's a great question. What do we do now?

"Well, I guess we have no choice but to bust down the door and—"

But as I reach for the doorknob, I notice the shadow beneath the door disappear. That's weird? Did the sun shift? Or... uh-oh. "Duck!"

Just then, the door BURSTS off its hinges!

I grab Selfie and Skunk Girl and hit the ground as the door goes flying over us! The next thing I know, Night Owl comes riding out the front door on one of her shadow slides!

"There she goes!" Pinball yells, pointing to the sky as Night Owl disappears over the house across the street. "She's getting away!"

"Not on my watch!" Grace says, taking off into the air after her.

But something tells me I can't just leave this up to Grace, so I concentrate hard and duplicate her power. And then I go airborne!

"Hey!" Skunk Girl calls out. "What about us?"

"Wait here!" I yell. "We'll be back!"

I have to say, one of the coolest parts of being a Meta Manipulator is copying the powers of a Flyer like Grace. There's nothing in the world like zooming through the air at supersonic speed, especially when you're chasing a villain. Unfortunately, it always takes me a few seconds to remember how to do it right.

So, after nearly crashing through a second-story window, sideswiping a brick chimney, and avoiding a head-on collision with a flock of geese, I'm finally stable enough to join the chase. Grace is way up ahead and she's nearly caught up to Night Owl, who is shooting solid shadow blasts back at Grace to shake her off her tail!

The good news is she doesn't see me coming. The bad news is that we're flying directly over Keystone City, which means this could get messy if we don't take her down quickly. But Night Owl is going really fast, and if Grace can't catch her I'm pretty sure I won't either.

Time for plan B.

I veer left and head for downtown. If I can circle those office buildings I'll surprise Night Owl from the other side. But as I loop around it dawns on me that if we collide in mid-air we could end up going splat. So, I come up with a new idea to end this sky chase. I'll just need to act quickly so no one gets hurt.

As I clear the last building I spot Night Owl and Grace heading right for me. I hover in the air, concentrate hard, and send a wave of negation energy right at Night Owl.

"You!" she says as soon as she sees me, her brown eyes growing wide. "I should have known it was—Hey, what's happening?"

Just then, the darkness coming from her fingertips dries up and her shadow slide dissipates into nothing. She hangs there for a second, shocked and grasping at empty air, and then she falls like a rock. But before I can go after her—

"I've got her," Grace calls out, but then disaster strikes as Grace flies right through my negation zone! The next thing I know, Grace screams and starts falling too!

Holy smokes! We're hundreds of feet in the air! And

that's when I realize I'm tapping into Grace's power. If I didn't store enough to keep myself afloat we're all toast!

I've got to act fast!

I divebomb after them and reach Grace first, grabbing her tightly around the waist.

"Remember that black cloud thing?" I shout.

"If we survive this," she shouts back, "I'm gonna kill you."

That's fair. But first I've got to catch Night Owl. The only problem is that I'm running out of gas. In fact, I can actually feel my flight power waning! I've got to motor!

"Stretch out your legs!" I yell at Grace. "We need to be more aerodynamic!"

Grace kicks out her arms and legs and we pick up more speed. That's great but I've got another problem. Where will we land? Grabbing Night Owl will just add more weight and I won't have enough power left to get the three of us safely to the ground.

That's when I spot the police station below. It's just a few stories above the ground, but it might be my best target. I stretch my legs and make an extra push. But based on how Night Owl is falling I think she's passed out. That's not going to be helpful, but we're closing in on the police station.

Last chance!

I accelerate with everything I've got and grab Night Owl around the waist. She flops limply against me and I pull up with everything I've got. Suddenly, we clear the roofline of the police station and tumble over one another. My body pounds against the cement, and by the time we stop rolling it feels like I've been run over by a fleet of trucks.

"G-Grace?" I call out, lying on my back and trying to catch my breath. "A-Are you okay?"

"Y-Yeah," she says, lying face down with a bruised cheek and bloody nose. "I'm just dandy, thanks."

"I'm so sorry," I say, "I guess I didn't think that through."

"Really?" Grace says. "I couldn't tell. By the way, my birthday present from you just got a whole lot bigger. How's the girl?"

I crawl over to Night Owl relieved to see she's still breathing. And she doesn't look too beat up which probably means Grace and I broke her fall.

"Night Owl?" I say, leaning over her. "It's Epic Zero. Are you okay? Can you hear me?"

Slowly, her eyelids flutter, and when she opens her eyes she says, "W-What did you do to me?"

"I negated your powers," I say.

"B-But you saved me," she says. "Why?"

"Because I told you I'm a hero," I say. "That's what heroes do."

"Right," she says. "I thought you and your friends were villains coming to attack me. I thought you were going to kill me. That's why I ran."

"What? No," I say. "We weren't trying to kill you.

We wanted to know what you know about a guy named Tormentus."

"Tormentus?" she says. "I-I don't know anyone called Tormentus."

Um, what? That wasn't the answer I was expecting.

"Are you sure?" I ask. "Maybe he gave you a different name, but he's got yellow eyes and purple skin. He told you he would trade information on how to get our parents back in exchange for your soul."

"What?" she says. "No, I never met anyone like that."

I look into her confused eyes and I know she's telling me the truth. So, that means this was all a mistake, because if Night Owl wasn't the one who sold her soul to Tormentus then who did? I mean, we were the only two who knew about the giant Powerbot toy.

"So, wait," Grace says, limping over. "Are you telling me this was all for nothing? I almost died for nothing? Dude, you're nothing but bad luck!"

Bad. Luck?

And that's when it hits me.

We went after the wrong Meta girl.

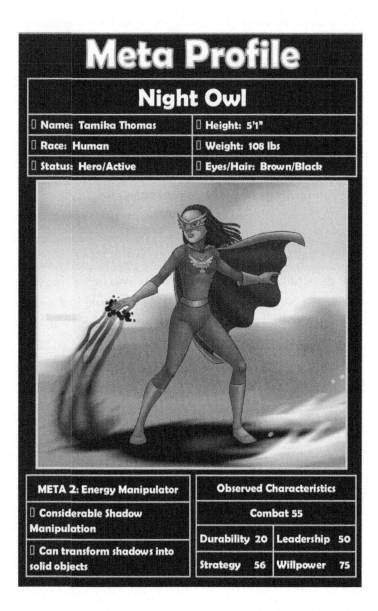

Meta Profile

Night Owl

▢ Name: Tamika Thomas	▢ Height: 5'1"
▢ Race: Human	▢ Weight: 108 lbs
▢ Status: Hero/Active	▢ Eyes/Hair: Brown/Black

META 2: Energy Manipulator	Observed Characteristics	
▢ Considerable Shadow Manipulation	Combat 55	
▢ Can transform shadows into solid objects	Durability 20	Leadership 50
	Strategy 56	Willpower 75

ELEVEN

I CAN'T REST FOR A SECOND

"Don't be so hard on yourself," Selfie says.

That's easy for her to say. After all, she didn't nearly get her sister killed chasing the wrong suspect. After that embarrassing episode, I'm surprised anyone is still willing to listen to me. But Next Gen considers me to be their leader so I've got to bounce back. And that's why we're back on the Waystation starting at square one.

"Do you think you can find her?" Selfie asks as I type into the Meta Monitor.

"I know I can," I say, and this time I'm convinced I'm after the right person.

Haywire.

The more I think about it, the more I realize how everything points back to her. Tormentus told me the person who sold him that soul was a 'she.' And Haywire was at the Keystone City Zoo with me and Night Owl. I can still see the determination in her eyes when she told me she'll do anything to find her parents and be a great hero, even without Next Gen. So, would she make a pact with Tormentus to get what she wanted?

I'm thinking yes.

And I'm kicking myself for not figuring it out sooner. We're losing time by the second. Especially if we're going to save—

"Epic Zero?" Grace says, entering the Monitor Room with an ice bag over her bruised cheek, "can I speak with you privately?"

"Oh, sure," Selfie says, shooting me a concerned look. "I'll just step out."

"Thanks," Grace says. "I suggest you go down to the Galley. Pinball and Dog-Gone were arguing over some leftover fried chicken and it was getting nasty."

"Right," Selfie says. "Will do. See you later."

As Selfie leaves, I'm pretty sure I know what Grace is doing here. She's probably going to let me have it. I mean, she has every right to be angry with me after the Night Owl incident. So, I brace myself, and as soon as Selfie's footsteps stop echoing down the stairway, we both blurt out—

"Grace, I'm sorry."

"Elliott, I'm scared."

"Wait, what?" I say, totally confused. "What did you

just say?"

"I-I said I'm scared," Grace says, her eyes welling up. "I mean, I turn fifteen tomorrow and I don't know what'll happen to me. I could vanish off the face of the Earth, never to be seen again. I don't know what to do."

As I watch tears stream down her cheeks I'm taken aback. I don't think I've ever seen Grace cry like, ever. She's always the tough one. The strong one.

"I-I miss Mom and Dad," she says, her voice cracking, "but I don't want to end up like them. We've got to find them. We've got to find out what happened to them and stop it from happening to others, including me." She pauses and wipes her tears away with her forearm. "Sorry, you know I'm not normally like this, but you're the only one I can talk to."

"N-No," I say, "it's okay. I'm glad you're telling me. Look, I'm doing everything I can to figure this out. And I'm sorry about all of those mistakes I made. I guess I am a bonehead sometimes."

"No, Elliott," she says, putting her hand on my shoulder, "you're not a bonehead. Well, not all the time. Look, if anyone is going to solve this mystery it's you. You're more patient than me, and I hate to admit it, but you're a better thinker too. Hey, you're not recording me saying this stuff, are you?"

"What?" I say, pretending to move my hand away from the dashboard. "No, but maybe I should."

"I'm counting on you, squirt," Grace says, her voice

sounding more like herself. "Got it?"

"Yeah," I say. "Look, as often as I joke about it I don't want you disappearing on me. Now Dog-Gone on the other hand…"

"Ha," she says. "He's your best friend so I don't believe that for a second. Anyway, did you find out anything about that Tormentus guy?"

"Nothing," I answer. The first thing I did when we got back to the Waystation was look him up on the Meta Monitor, but there's no profile. It's like he doesn't even exist."

"And Haywire?" she asks.

"The Meta Monitor is doing its thing," I say. "Fortunately, I was able to put in the coordinates of the places I know she used her powers but they're not active readings anymore. Night Owl was really active so she was easy to find. Hopefully, Haywire has been active recently."

"Speaking of Night Owl," Grace says, "she seems kind of reserved. She's not really saying much to anyone."

"Can you blame her?" I say. "I mean, I nearly killed her only fifteen minutes ago."

"Fair," Grace says. "But she's still an odd bird."

Well, I agree with her about that. I invited Night Owl to join us and she declined at first but then changed her mind right before we left. I've seen her in action and I know she'll be a big help. Hopefully, she'll stick around.

"Alert! Alert! Alert!" the Meta Monitor blares.

"Here it comes!" I say.

"Meta 1 disturbance. Repeat: Meta 1 disturbance. Power signature identified as Haywire. Alert! Alert! Alert! Meta 1 disturbance. Power signature identified as Haywire."

"Where's the signal coming from?" Grace asks. "What's the location?"

I look at the monitor and do a double take.

"Um, is that right?" I ask. "Because it says it's coming from Safari Park."

***

"I love Safari Park," Pinball says. "My parents took me and my brother there a few years ago. It's the largest animal park in the whole world."

"Great," Skunk Girl says, "maybe we can leave you there when we're done."

"Actually," Pinball says, "being around you is kind of like being at Safari Park, especially if you're standing downwind."

"Can you guys please stop?" Selfie says. "The constant digs are just getting annoying."

"You can say that again," Grace says. "How much longer until we're there?"

"We'll be there in one minute," I say, checking the Freedom Flyer's radar. But the thing I can't figure out is why Haywire is even at Safari Park. I mean, the last place

I saw her was at the Keystone City Zoo, which is over a thousand miles north of Safari Park. And come to think of it, what's with the animal theme? I'm guessing this is all connected, I just don't know how.

"Anyway," Pinball says, "Safari Park is so enormous you can't do the whole thing in one day. They have all of these different lands inside, like Elephant Land, Big Cat Land, and Giraffe Land. Each land has its own animal preserve you can tour, amazing animal shows, and they even let you feed some of the animals at designated times. Plus, they also have Fun Land where you can ride rollercoasters and stuff. It's super awesome. Have you been there, Night Owl?"

"Nope," Night Owl says. "Can't say I have."

"You'd like it," Pinball says. "They have owls you can hang with."

"I'll keep that in mind," Night Owl says.

Well, Grace was right. Night Owl is acting a bit reserved. She probably just needs some time to warm up. After all, we're still strangers to her. But one thing I do know is that she's as committed to this mission as we are. She told me she wants to get her parents back. And after our little case of mistaken identity, she also wants to catch Haywire.

Just then, we fly over a massive, well-manicured park that stretches for miles. Well, I've never been to Safari Park myself but that must be it. Looking down I can see large animals moving through the park but something seems off. That's when I realize the animals aren't confined to designated areas. They're roaming lose all over the park! It's just like the zoo! Someone set the animals free!

"Is that an elephant walking down Main Street?" Selfie asks.

"Guys?" Pinball says.

"And look at the white rhino," Skunk Girl says. "It's crushing that picnic table."

"Um, guys," Pinball says.

"Does anyone else see a polar bear knocking over a vending machine?" Grace asks.

"Guys!" Pinball yells.

"What?" Skunk Girl says. "What is it?"

"Th-There's a… robot behind us," Pinball says, pointing over his shoulder.

THOOM!

Suddenly, our left wing explodes and the Freedom Flyer tilts off course! I peer into the rearview mirror to see Pinball is right, there is a robot flying behind us! But it's not just any robot, it's another giant Powerbot! And it's got us dead in its sights!

"Hold on!" I yell.

I rotate sideways just as another missile shoots by, but my dashboard is lit up like a Christmas tree. We've lost a thruster and smoke is pouring out of my wing!

We're going down!

"Keep your eyes on the road!" Grace yells.

I grit my teeth and try to level us out, but the steering column isn't cooperating. If I don't land this puppy fast that bucket of bolts will blow us clear out of the sky. I look for the closest place to touch down when—

"He's aiming at us again!" Pinball yells.

"Not if I can help it," Night Owl says.

Then, she unbuckles herself, setting off the safety alarm.

"What are you doing back there?" I call out.

"Saving us," she says. And then she lifts the large shadow from beneath Pinball and projects it through the rear window, enveloping the Powerbot in darkness. And when she closes her fist the robot shatters into a gazillion pieces.

"Whoa!" Skunk Girl says. "I didn't know you could do that!"

"I think I have a new love," Pinball mutters.

"That's the best news I've heard all day," Grace says.

I knew Night Owl would come in handy, but we're not out of the woods yet because we're coming in hot. I engage the landing gear and pull back on the throttle with everything I've got to level us off.

"Should I drive?" Grace yells, gripping her armrests so tightly her knuckles are white.

"Nope," I say, "I've got it."

By now I've had more experience with emergency landings than I'd care to admit, but I've never had one that required dodging free-range animals. I spot the longest strip of roadway available, and then angle the Freedom Flyer toward it. This isn't going to be easy.

"Hold on tight!" I yell, trying to sound confident but my voice betrays me. I drop the back of the Freedom Flyer and Dog-Gone YIPS as the wheels touch the ground hard. We're halfway there! But as I lay down the front—

"Ostrich!" Grace yells.

Ostrich? Suddenly, a giant bird jumps in front of us and I swerve right, just missing it except for a few feathers that get pinned to the windshield. I quickly pull left to level off the Freedom Flyer and slam on the brakes. Selfie grabs Night Owl as everyone flies forward in their seatbelts as we SCREECH to a stop, just a few feet away from a confused pack of porcupines.

That's when I realize I'm completely covered in sweat. And that I also despise ostriches.

"Nice driving," Skunk Girl says, "now who's going to clean-up Dog-Gone's barf?"

"Not it," Pinball says, his finger on his nose.

I look back at Dog-Gone's green face and the mess on the floor and now I know who won the battle over the leftover fried chicken. Well, at least that's one mystery solved.

"We'll deal with it later," I say, unbuckling my seatbelt. "We've lost any element of surprise. We've got to get out of here and find Haywire before she takes off on us. Next Gen—Let's Get Even!"

"Um, is that your new battle cry?" Skunk Girl asks as she hops out. "Because it's super lame."

"I guess not," I say. "Let's just go."

But as soon as I step out of the Freedom Flyer I realize we won't be going far.

Because we're surrounded by Powerbots!

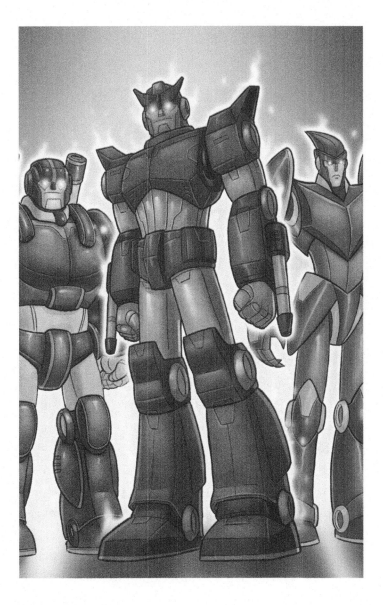

TWELVE

I GET QUITE THE SURPRISE

This is not good.

I mean, first, we're shot out of the air by a flying Powerbot, and now we're surrounded by dozens more. They're big, mean, and aiming their assorted weaponry right at us. I look at Night Owl who has her hands in the air like the rest of us. I guess there's too many of them even for her.

Of course, my powers don't work on robots so I'm crippled with uselessness. As I stare into the red, unblinking eyes of the Powerbot in front of me it triggers a memory. You know, I think I actually had that one as a toy. His name is Star-warp or something like that. I remember him having a heat-seeking missile-arm which, coincidentally, seems to be pointed right at me.

I still can't figure out where these giant-sized toys came from, let alone what their purpose is. But right now, I need to do something before this turns ugly. I'm about to open my mouth when Star-warp pushes his missile-arm hard into my chest!

"Ow!" I say. "Back off!"

But the Powerbot doesn't move.

"Your name is Star-warp, isn't it?" I ask. "Or is it Warp-star? Anyway, we're not looking for trouble here. We were just passing overhead when one of your guys decided to blow us out of the sky. So, let's say we skip the obligatory fight scene and go for some ice cream and motor oil?"

But Star-warp doesn't respond.

"Okay, I get it," I say. "If you're not into motor oil we could go for premium gas instead?"

Then, his eyes start pulsing.

"Epic Zero!" Selfie calls out. "He's gonna shoot!"

She's right! But before I can move, Star-warp's torso swivels and his missile-arm fires! THOOM! I shield my face as robot-parts explode everywhere. But when I look back up I realize he's blown three of his buddies to smithereens!

But why? What's going on?

Suddenly, all of the robots aim at one another.

"Everyone down!" Grace yells.

We hit the deck as a barrage of crossfire flashes overhead. THOOM! THOOM! I curl into a ball as more robot-parts shower my body, and when the onslaught finally stops I look up to find smoldering Powerbots lying all around us.

What the heck just happened? Why did they take each other out? But I don't have to wait long for an answer, because suddenly a girl says—

"So, do you think I'm Next Gen material now?"

I turn to find Haywire standing over us with her arms crossed and a scowl on her face. And as I look into her eyes I can tell that something has changed—and maybe not for the better.

"Wait, did you do this?" Skunk Girl asks. "Because I thought you couldn't control your powers."

"That was the old me," Haywire says. "But things are different now. In fact, things are so different that I don't need your little team anymore. So, now that I've shown you what you passed up on, I suggest you losers crawl back into your shuttle and leave."

"Well, that's harsh," Pinball says.

Harsh is right. This is definitely not the Haywire I remember. I mean, when she tried out for our team she was determined but sincere. Now she's got an edge, and I don't doubt for a minute where it came from.

Tormentus.

"Life is harsh, isn't it?" Haywire says. "Now I've got a job to do and I don't need you getting in my way. So, you can either leave on your own, or I can provide a little motivation to help you on your way."

"Now hang on there, missy," Grace starts.

"Wait," I say, cutting her off. "We'll go."

Grace shoots me a look but I know what I'm doing. Tormentus must have given Haywire better control of her powers in exchange for her soul, and that makes her extremely dangerous. I mean, just look at how easily she disposed of those Powerbots.

But I'm betting that's not all Tormentus gave her.

If he offered her the same deal he offered me, then I'm guessing Haywire knows who is doing all of this. Yet, my gut tells me she'll clam up if I confront her about her deal with Tormentus. She wants us to believe she got this powerful all on her own. So, this is going to take some delicate probing. I just need to get her talking. Maybe if I boost her ego she'll let something slip.

"I knew you'd be a great hero someday," I say.

"Not just a great hero," she says, "but the greatest of all time. And today I'm going to prove it."

"I bet you will," I say. "But if you don't mind me asking, how exactly will you prove you're the greatest hero ever? Maybe we can help."

"Sorry, but no," Haywire says. "I'm taking him down all on my own."

"Him?" I say. "Who exactly is 'him?'"

But instead of answering me, her eyes narrow. "You're trying to trick me, aren't you? You're trying to get me to tell you stuff. Well, that's not happening. So, here's your last warning. Leave or else."

"I pick 'or else,'" Night Owl says.

"Wait!" I call out, but it's too late.

Night Owl pulls a shadow from beneath the Freedom Flyer and launches it at Haywire when it suddenly reverses direction and wraps around Night Owl herself!

"My, how unlucky," Haywire says with an evil grin.

Night Owl screams as the shadow squeezes her like a tube of toothpaste. For a second, I debate negating Haywire's power but who knows if it will work. Plus, if I do that she'll never cooperate with us. Instead, I've got a new plan. I just need her to release Night Owl.

"Stop!" I call out. "We'll go. Just let her free first."

Haywire hesitates before relenting. "Fine," she says. Then, the shadow slips away dumping Night Owl to the ground. "Take your lame new recruit and go."

"I'm not... their new recruit," Night Owl says, breathing heavily and holding her ribs.

"Let's go," I say, helping Night Owl to her feet.

"Can the Freedom Flyer even fly?" Pinball asks. "Look at the wing. Half of it is destroyed."

Well, he's right about that. "If we stay low we should be able to clear Safari Park," I say. Then, I turn to Haywire and say, "Good luck."

"I won't need it," she says, watching us board.

I leave the hatch open and when everyone gets to their seats, I stand up and offer Grace the controls. "You take it from here."

"Me?" she says. "Why, where are you going?"

"After Haywire," I whisper. "Listen, she's too unpredictable to fight head-on and it's my responsibility as leader to keep my team safe. But I'm gonna take Dog-Gone and follow her invisibly. You fly out of here so it looks like we've all left and I'll radio you later when I find out what's happening."

"Is that a good idea?" Grace whispers back.

"Do you have a better one?" I ask.

"Hey," Skunk Girl says, "where's Night Owl?"

I look back and Night Owl is gone. She must have snuck out in the shadows!

Just. Freaking. Wonderful.

Well, I can't worry about her now because I'll lose Haywire's trail. "C'mon, boy," I say to Dog-Gone.

"Where are you going?" Selfie asks.

"You guys are in good hands with Glory Girl," I say. "Listen to everything she says. I'll catch up later."

"Hey, be careful," Grace says.

"I will," I say. "And remember to overcompensate on the steering column to account for the wing—"

"I've got it," Grace says. "Don't do anything stupid."

"You too," I say, and then smile as I borrow Dog-Gone's power and we exit the Freedom Flyer invisibly. As Grace closes the hatch behind me and takes off overhead, I watch Haywire turn satisfied and head down a pathway. Great, she didn't notice us, but I guess she didn't notice Night Owl either.

I look up as the Freedom Flyer skims the trees, leaving a trail of smoke behind it. Grace is a good pilot so they'll be okay, but now I've got to do my part. The only thing is, I can't see Dog-Gone when he turned invisible.

"Where are you?" I whisper, reaching out for him. Then, I feel a wet nose against my palm. "Okay, follow that girl. But don't make any noise because we need to see where she's going. And no growling."

Dog-Gone brushes past me and we're off. As we run, I check out Safari Park for the first time. It looks like a fun place to visit, you know, if you had a normal life and all. Suddenly, I'm dodging all sorts of exotic birds strutting across the grounds and realize we've ventured into Feather Land. That's when I have a momentary flash of panic. What if Dog-Gone is hunting peacocks right now?

But when I reach out with my powers I find him way up ahead. As long as he's hot on Haywire's trail I just need to stay connected to him. His signal leads me over a bridge with a sign that reads: *Big Cat Land*.

Well, let's hope he's around here somewhere.

"Dog-Gone?" I whisper. "Are you here?"

Suddenly, there's a low GRRROOOWWWLLLL.

"Um, Dog-Gone?"

But as I round the corner I find myself face-to-face with a four-legged creature that's definitely not my mutt. Now, I'm no zoologist, but by the muscular body and cat-like head, I'd bet my bottom dollar that's a puma. And even though I'm invisible, its nose is working overtime—which means he knows I'm here!

"Um, nice kitty cat," I say, my heart racing.

But as the puma steps towards me, newspaper headlines flash before my eyes: *Invisible Boy Presumed Eaten by Puma. Remains Never Found.* Or even: *Kid Hero Gives Puma Indigestion. Puma Recovers After Full Bottle of Antacids.*

Just then, the puma leaps, and I open my mouth to scream for my life when the cat is suddenly wrapped inside a blanket of darkness. I've been saved! And as the puma struggles in vain to get out my savior appears.

"I know you're there, Epic Zero," Night Owl says, stepping off her shadow slide behind the puma. "I've been following your footsteps since you left the Freedom Flyer. Rescuing you is becoming a habit."

"Well, you know what they say," I remark while turning visible. "Third times the charm. But enough about me, what are you doing here? Why didn't you stay on the Freedom Flyer?"

"And miss my shot at revenge on Haywire?" Night Owl says. "No chance. And what about you?"

"I want to find out what she knows to get the grown-ups back," I say.

"Well, that makes two of us," she says.

"Then I guess we're joining forces on this one," I say, offering my hand. "Deal?"

"Deal," she says, shaking it. "Now let's find Haywire. She could be anywhere by now."

"Don't worry, I've got a mole on her tail," I say.

"Then this time ride with me," Night Owl says, forming a shadow slide and offering her hand.

I climb up and realize it's super solid.

"Hold on tight," she says, "and tell me where to go."

I grab her waist and we're off! I have to say, I've never ridden a shadow before, and it kind of feels like surfing through the air. Under ordinary circumstances, I'm sure this would be a blast, but right now I need to focus on staying connected to Dog-Gone while not falling off.

Suddenly, I see all kinds of rides below and realize we must be over Fun Land, the amusement park section. There's a Ferris wheel, a water flume, and an absolutely massive roller coaster track going through the middle of a fake mountain with a sign that reads: *Expedition Danger. Ride at Your Own Risk.* And Dog-Gone's signal is coming in strong at the base of the mountain!

"Down there," I say, pointing to the spot. But then I see Haywire standing by the Expedition Danger entrance. "Wait! Pull up! She's right there!"

Night Owl raises her shadow slide just as Haywire disappears through the entrance. We hover in the air for a few seconds until the coast is clear.

"Okay, you can take us down now," I say.

Night Owl lowers the slide to ground level and I jump off. "Dog-Gone," I whisper, "where are you?"

Just then, Dog-Gone appears out of thin air with his

tongue hanging out and tail wagging.

"Good boy," I say, rubbing his muzzle. "Of course, you did leave me to die at the paws of that puma, but at least you stuck to your assignment. Now I've got to see what Haywire is up to. Night Owl, follow—"

But when I turn around, she's gone again.

Well, so much for teamwork.

Time to go, but maybe I shouldn't bring Dog-Gone with me. I mean, this will definitely be dangerous, and while he followed instructions earlier, he's not exactly the most obedient dog on the planet. "Dog-Gone, stay here," I say, "and stay out of sight."

Dog-Gone furrows his brow and cocks an ear.

Uh-oh. I feel a bribe coming on. I don't have time for this. "Fine," I say. "You listen and I'll give you all the treats you want."

Dog-Gone sticks out his tongue and disappears.

Well, I'm not proud of caving to his demands but that ought to hold him. Besides, I've got more important things to do. So, I borrow his invisibility power and head for the ride entrance, passing by a warning sign that reads:

Persons with the following conditions should not ride: (1) Heart Conditions. (2) Back, Neck, or Similar Physical Conditions. (3) Pregnant Mothers. (4) Motion Sickness. (5) Other Medical Conditions that may be Aggravated by this Ride.

Funny, for some reason I was hoping it'd say: *(6) Or any Kid Wearing a Cape.* But no such luck so I press on.

The entrance to the Expedition Danger ride is dark

and narrow, and I follow a wooden pathway lined with frayed, waist-high ropes. The walls are covered with rusty climbing equipment and yellowed newspapers warning about a man-eating Yeti. Well, this ride definitely makes you feel like you're about to go on a treacherous expedition—which in my case isn't too far from the truth. As I move through the queue I keep an eye out for Haywire and Night Owl, but I don't see them anywhere.

Then, the pathway goes up.

About a hundred feet later, I walk beneath a red, hand-painted sign that says: *Expedition Danger: Proceed at Your Own Risk.* The next thing I know, the wall decorations give way to mountain scenery as a chilly breeze whips across my face. I keep climbing up, past a pile of fake goat bones, and around a steep bend until I reach a plateau. Funny, but I do feel out of breath, like I'm standing at a crazy high altitude.

Then, voices echo through the chamber—

"I've been waiting for you," comes a voice that sounds strangely familiar.

"Bring my parents back!" Haywire yells.

Even though I'm invisible, I get down on my hands and knees and peer over the edge of the plateau. The first thing I see is a rickety, wooden staircase leading down to a row of empty roller coaster cars. Well, I guess that's where the actual ride starts. But that's not what grabs my attention because Haywire is standing on the other side of the cars with her back to me. And she's facing a rather enormous man sitting in a gold throne in front of a fake, golden temple.

That's strange, why does that guy look so familiar?

But as I take a closer look a chill runs down my spine and I gasp in disbelief.

He has white skin, white hair, and giant muscles.

B-But that's impossible. I mean, it couldn't be.

Then, his blue eyes blaze red and I feel sick to my stomach. Because that's not a man at all.

It's… Siphon!

Meta Profile

Siphon

▢ Name: Siphon		▢ Height: 6'5"	
▢ Race: Human		▢ Weight: 1,050 lbs	
▢ Status: Villain/Inactive		▢ Eyes/Hair: Blue/White	

META 3: Meta Manipulator	Observed Characteristics	
▢ Extreme Power Duplication	Combat 100	
▢ WARNING: It is not known if Siphon can reach Meta 4 power levels like his father Meta-Taker	Durability 100	Leadership 40
	Strategy 80	Willpower 90

THIRTEEN

I BREAK A DATE WITH DESTINY

My eyes must be playing tricks on me.

I mean, it's just not possible. There's no way Siphon could be sitting there. But when I blink and open my eyes again, there he is.

But how? The last time I saw Siphon was back on Arena World where he sacrificed himself to put an end to Order and Chaos. By using the opposing powers of the Orb of Oblivion and the Building Block, Siphon blew all of them, not to mention Arena World, into nothingness.

There's no way he could have survived that.

Could he?

As I think back to that horrific day, I realize I never actually saw Siphon die. Just before everything went nuts, he used Wind Walker's power to wormhole me to safety. So, all of this time I just assumed he was dead. But maybe

I was wrong. Except, it just doesn't make any sense.

"I know you did it!" Haywire yells at Siphon. "I know you're responsible for making the grown-ups disappear! Now bring them back, or else!"

"You have a unique power, don't you?" Siphon says, closing his eyes and breathing in deep. "I can sense it within you."

"Yeah?" Haywire says. "Well, if you don't tell me the truth you'll feel my power firsthand, bozo!"

Uh-oh. Haywire may be stronger than she was, but she has no idea who she's dealing with. Siphon is a Meta 3 Meta Manipulator just like his father, Meta-Taker, which means he can duplicate the powers of others, including multiple Metas at the same time.

My mind flashes back to the first time I scuffled with Siphon back at that abandoned warehouse. I was much less experienced then and he would have destroyed me if he weren't transported to Arena World by that strange orange energy. I was lucky, but I can't count on lightning striking twice.

"If you fancy a sparring partner," Siphon says, standing up from his throne and waving his left hand with a grand flourish, "I'm at your service."

But as he flicks his wrist, something reflects off his finger and I do a double take. He's wearing a silver ring! But that can't be a coincidence, can it? Because if that ring is the silver Ring of Suffering, then things have just gone from bad to much, much worse.

I need to get a closer look.

I step carefully onto the rickety staircase, which shakes under the weight of my foot. Great. The last thing I need is to give myself away. Yet, I'm going to need help because stopping Siphon alone is downright difficult. But stopping Siphon while he's wearing a Ring of Suffering is freaking impossible! I reach for my transmitter to contact the team when—

"I sense we have a guest," Siphon says.

I stop in my tracks. Um, what?

"Perhaps we should welcome him," he continues.

"What are you talking about?" Haywire asks.

"There's someone here I know all too well," Siphon says, breathing in deep with his arms extended to his sides. "Isn't that right, Epic Zero?"

What? How did he know I was here? Then, I remember he can sense Meta power, just like he did when I first met him. Well, I guess it's no use being invisible now. I just need to look more confident than I feel.

"I'm here," I say, turning visible and striking a heroic pose with my hands on my hips. "But the real question is, what are you doing here? I thought you were dead."

"So did I," Siphon says, "but fortunately, I'm not."

"But how is that possible?" I ask. "There was a massive explosion. Nobody could have survived that."

"Hold on there, buddy," Haywire interjects, pointing at me. "I'll be the one asking all the questions around here. I told you this guy was mine and mine alone."

"You're being rude to our guest," Siphon says to Haywire. "I don't think I like you."

"So what?" Haywire says. "I came here to get answers and I'm not leaving until you—"

BOOM!

Siphon socks her with unbelievable speed and Haywire flies across the room, crashing into a rock wall.

"Haywire!" I yell, running down the staircase. "What did you do that for?"

"She annoyed me," Siphon says, sitting back down on his throne. "I no longer tolerate things that annoy me."

I kneel next to Haywire and she's still breathing but out cold. I can't believe Siphon sucker punched her. I mean, he was bad when I first met him, but he was a hero in the end. What happened to him?

But as he cracks his knuckles I get a good look at the silver ring on his finger. It has a lightning bolt on its face, just like the bronze ring in the Trophy Room! I feel sick to my stomach.

And that's when I remember Beezle's Meta profile. It said the Djinn Three can control the desires of their hosts. Is that what's going on? Is Beezle mind-controlling Siphon? Is that why he's acting so strange?

"Look, we were friends, remember?" I say, standing up. "I'm glad to see you again, but you have to tell me why you're doing this."

"*Friends?*" Siphon says, staring at me oddly. "I don't

have any friends. I wasn't ever allowed to have friends."

"Well, I consider you a friend," I say. "You saved my life. You even told me to remember you as a hero."

"Yeah," Siphon says with a chuckle. "I guess I did say that, didn't I? Imagine, me, a hero? Well, it wasn't in the cards. And once I came back I decided to be true to myself. I guess the apple doesn't fall far from the tree."

I don't know what he's talking about, but he's clearly not himself.

"But how did you come back?" I ask. "I still don't understand how you're even alive?"

"Just lucky I guess," Siphon says. "You see, after I sent you away, a fraction of a second before I pulled Order and Chaos together, it was like time stood still. Except the funny thing was, I wasn't on Arena World anymore, but sitting at a table inside a dark room. And across from me was this purple-skinned guy who welcomed me to his 'office.'"

Purple-skinned guy? A chill runs down my spine.

"I'd never seen him before so I asked him if I was dead." Siphon continues. "And he said that was up to me. He said I could choose death if I wanted, or he could save me and send me back to Earth if I was willing to bargain with him. He said all he wanted in exchange for my life was—"

"—your soul?" I say, finishing his sentence.

"Yeah," Siphon says, his eyebrows raised. "How'd you know that?"

"Because he tried the same thing with me," I say. "He calls himself Tormentus. But I didn't take him up on his offer."

"Well, I did," Siphon says. "After all, what did I have to lose? I was a goner anyway. But first I asked him why he even wanted my soul. What was he going to do with it? He said he needed powerful souls for a war he was going to start. But when I asked him who he was fighting he wouldn't tell me. But what did I care? So, I agreed to his deal on the spot, and then asked him what I was supposed to do next. Do you know what he told me?"

"Um, no," I say.

"He said I should go fulfill my destiny," Siphon says. "And the next thing I knew I was back on Earth. I never learned what happened on Arena World after I was gone. I figured I was pulling Order and Chaos together so hard they had to touch, but I didn't think you or any of the others survived. Then, I saw you on the news a few weeks later and I knew you got out okay."

"But why didn't you try to contact me?" I ask. "I could have helped you."

"Nah," he says. "No one can help me. I'm a lost cause. My dad made sure of that."

"But you're not your dad," I say. "Your dad was pure evil, but you're not like him. I mean, I've seen what you're capable of. You have so much potential."

"Wasted potential," Siphon says. "So, I kind of wandered around aimlessly for a while trying to figure things out. I mean, I couldn't understand why I got a second chance? What good did I ever do to even deserve it? Was I supposed to become a hero and try to right my dad's wrongs? Was that my destiny? Or was I supposed to honor my dad by picking up the torch he left behind? I couldn't decide what to do. And then I found this."

He turns the silver ring around his finger.

"This ring was a sign," Siphon says. "I found it just sitting there in the back of an alley. Like it was waiting just for me. It had this strange lightning bolt on it and I felt like I had to put it on. And when I did, well, that's when my destiny became clear. Isn't that right, Beezle?"

Just then, the ring sparks with electricity, and the next thing I know out comes a giant, yellow spirit-like thing that looks like a cross between a human and a troll! I crane my neck as it swells to twenty feet in size and circles Siphon like a cobra protecting its young.

I-It's Beezle!

The evil genie looks down at me with yellow eyes and a sinister grin. Well, I guess I finally found him. The thing is, now that he's actually here I don't feel like sticking around. But I can't bolt because I know there's more to the story. And I have a funny feeling I'm about to find out what it is.

"So, um, if you don't mind me asking," I say, "now that you have your own evil genie and all, what exactly is your destiny?"

"To rule," Siphon says. "After all, Beezle called me

'master' and I liked the sound of that. And then he told me I could have three wishes. Isn't that right, Beezle?"

"Yes, master," Beezle says, his voice cold and gritty, like fingernails scraping a chalkboard.

"Oh," I say. "And you didn't wish for world peace?"

"No," Siphon says. "I wished for world domination, all thanks to you."

"Me?" I say. "What did I do?"

"You told me the truth about my dad," Siphon says. "You made me realize he lied to me my entire life. When he was around he said it was us against the world. But he never told me who he really was or what he was really doing. And when he disappeared, I was on my own. I couldn't even get an orphanage to take me in. When I took off my hood, the lady screamed and slammed the door in my face. I was living on the streets, scrounging for food and shelter. And the older kids, runaways themselves, wouldn't help me. They just made fun of me for the way I looked. They called me a savage. A beast. They said no one would take me in and I'd be on the streets forever like a dog. Well, I showed them. I showed them all."

He showed them? What does that mean?

And then it hits me.

"You wished the grown-ups away!" I blurt out. "You used one of Beezle's three wishes to get rid of them, didn't you?"

"Yeah," Siphon says. "I did. No adults or older kids

wanted me around so why would I want them around? My whole life feels like I've been trapped in a cage, like an animal. All of those people looking at me, laughing at me. But what makes them so special? I could crush them if I wanted to. So, now I'm choosing to be free. To be my true self. And I figure if I'm such a savage, then I'll live with animals instead of humans. That's why I came to Safari Park. Here, we can all be free."

Free?

Suddenly, the dots connect.

"You freed those animals at the zoo," I say. "You made those souped-up Powerbots too, didn't you? But why? Why would you waste a wish on that?"

"I didn't 'waste' anything," Siphon says, clearly annoyed. "When I was young my dad brought me some Powerbot toys he found in the trash, and those were the only friends I had. So, I got a whole bunch of them and made them into my army. They do all of my dirty work for me."

I-I can't believe it. Everything is coming together.

And Siphon is the one responsible!

But then I realize something.

"You said you had three wishes," I say. "What did you do with the third one?"

"That's easy," Siphon says. "I realized I can't pretend to be someone I'm not. My destiny was always right in front of my face. I'm no hero. After all, look who my father was. So, just before you and the annoying girl got here, I wished for the one thing I've always wanted the most."

"And... what's that?" I ask, afraid to hear the answer.

"To be a Meta 4," he says. "So, *friend*, if you think you're going to stop me you've got another thing coming."

Meta Profile

Beezle

Name: Beezle	Height: Variable
Race: Djinn	Weight: Variable
Status: Villain/Inactive	Eyes/Hair: Yellow/Bald

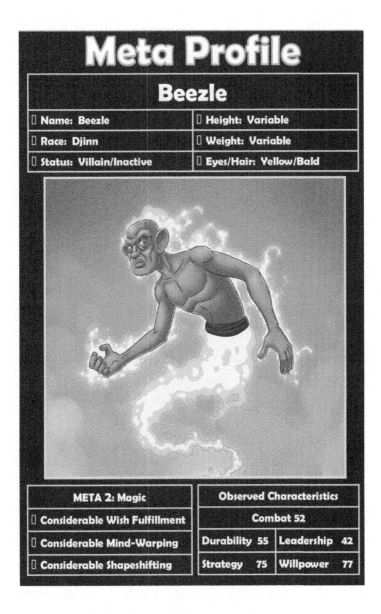

META 2: Magic	Observed Characteristics	
Considerable Wish Fulfillment	Combat 52	
Considerable Mind-Warping	Durability 55	Leadership 42
Considerable Shapeshifting	Strategy 75	Willpower 77

FOURTEEN

I FIGHT FOR MY LIFE

I'm in complete and total shock.

Not only did I just discover that Siphon is still alive, but I've also learned he's responsible for making the grown-ups disappear using one of Beezle's three wishes.

And now he's told me what he used his last wish for.

To become a META-FREAKING-4!

Which essentially means he's all-powerful. So, now I'm at a complete loss. I mean, I couldn't even stop him when he was just a Meta 3! I look down at the still unconscious Haywire and realize I'm on my own.

I'm not going to beat Siphon in battle, so I've got to find a way to get him to bring the grown-ups back without crushing me first. But then I realize something that gives me pause. Siphon said Beezle only granted him three wishes—and he's used them all already!

So, even if I somehow convince him to bring the grown-ups back, how would he do it? I mean, all the genies I've ever read about only come with three wishes. Will Beezle actually grant him a fourth wish? Something tells me I already know the answer to that one.

But no matter how impossible this situation looks, I can't just curl up into a ball. Right now, I'm the only one who knows the truth, and it's up to me to get my parents and the rest of the Freedom Force back. Not to mention the millions of other missing people.

No pressure.

Maybe I can convince him he's taken the wrong path—that he can still be a hero. I did it once before so I'll just have to do it again.

"Siphon, look," I say, "we don't have to fight. I know you think you had to follow in your father's footsteps, but it doesn't have to be that way. Let's just back up to the good versus evil fork-in-the-road and take the other path. Everyone deserves a second chance, and in your case, even a third."

"Nice try," Siphon says, cracking his very, very large knuckles, "but you're not talking me out of it this time. You see, now I know who I really am, so it's time we finished what we started the first time we met."

"The, um, first time we met?" I repeat nervously.

Suddenly, I flashback to when he nearly destroyed me in that abandoned warehouse. He borrowed all of the Ominous Eight's powers with ease and I barely escaped with my life. Then, I realize something.

Thank goodness I didn't call for help. If I did, then Siphon could use the powers of Grace and Next Gen against us! The less Metas around, the better shot I have.

"It's payback time," Siphon says. "And this time, I don't care what you say. I know you were responsible for my father's death, and now it's time for revenge. What's that saying, 'an eye for an eye?'"

"Oh, that ridiculous old saying?" I say, waving my hand dismissively. "I'm much more partial to, 'treat others how you want to be treated.'"

"Enough," Siphon says, his eyes flashing red.

This is it! I'm in for the fight of my life—literally!

How am I going to stop him!

As Siphon steps towards me, I glance up at Beezle who is smiling sinisterly overhead. And as my eyes follow Beezle's floating body, I realize he's still connected to the silver ring like a tetherball on a rope. And then a lightbulb goes off!

As long as Siphon is wearing the Ring of Suffering, he's under Beezle's influence. But what would happen if I got that ring off his finger?

"Sorry, *friend*," Siphon says. "I've enjoyed your little visit, but now it's time for you to die."

But before he takes a step, I concentrate and bathe him with negation power. The red embers in his eyes sputter for a few seconds before completely going out. But my victory is short-lived as he smiles and his eyes light right back up! Well, that didn't work. Not that I'm surprised because I couldn't negate his powers the first time we met.

Time for Plan B!

I reach out to duplicate his power, but instead of feeling the incredible, all-powerful surge of Meta 4 energy coursing through my veins, I feel absolutely nothing!

What gives?

"Is something wrong?" Siphon asks knowingly. "Perhaps you're feeling a bit powerless yourself? After all, I've just used your own negation power against you. Tell me, how does it feel to be a Zero?"

What? But the more I try to use my powers, the emptier I feel inside. I-I can't believe it. He's wiped my powers out!

"Even if I weren't a Meta 4," Siphon says, approaching me with a giant smirk across his mug, "your Meta Manipulation powers were never a match for mine. Now come take your punishment like a man."

"Well, that's the funny thing," I say, backing up quickly. "You got rid of all the men. I'm still a kid, remember?"

Just then, Siphon swings, and I duck as his fist swooshes overhead. Then, I nail him in the ribs with a roundhouse kick but he doesn't move.

"Augh!" I scream as pain shoots through my foot. Kicking him is like kicking a boulder. He's way too strong for me, powers, or no powers.

Suddenly, he grabs my collar and lifts me high into the air. As his hot breath blows in my face, I open my mouth to beg for my life but no words come out. He's squeezing my uniform so tight it's cutting off the circulation to my neck!

I feel woozy, and for a split second, instead of Siphon, I think I see Meta-Taker staring back at me. But then I blink and it's Siphon again. He's saying something but I can't really hear him. I... I'm having a... hard time breathing!

Siphon smiles as red energy crackles around his narrowing eyes. I'm... losing consciousness.

But then, a thick, black band wraps around Siphon's eyes and two more wrap around his wrists! Siphon yells something as his arms are pulled back with extreme force.

The next thing I know, I fall to the ground and land hard on my tailbone. Pain shoots up my backside as I try to catch my breath. But as much as I want to just sit here and recover, I can't because I've got to get my rescuer out of here.

"Night Owl!" I call out, my throat feeling hoarse.

"I could make a career out of saving you," she says, riding close to the hundred-foot-high ceiling.

"Get out of here!" I yell. "He'll copy your powers!"

Just then, Siphon breaks the shadows off his wrists and snaps the one covering his eyes in two. Then, he breathes in deep and spews a giant shadow tentacle out of his mouth straight toward Night Owl!

"Look out!" I yell, but it's too late because the tentacle wraps around Night Owl's shadow slide and pulls, shattering it into pieces!

Night Owl screams as she starts to plummet to the ground. I've got to do something! But Siphon negated my powers! I can't give up!

I concentrate harder than I've ever concentrated before, digging deep inside. I pull every last ember of Meta energy I can muster to the surface. And then I push, sweat trickling down my forehead, until I feel my Meta power moving, slowly at first, and then faster, until it explodes like water flowing through a dam. I-I did it!

But there's no time to celebrate. Got to be fast.

I copy Night Owl's power, grab the shadow beneath the staircase, and inflate it beneath her, breaking her fall with the biggest, fluffiest shadow marshmallow ever created. Night Owl lands in its cushiony center and bounces softly. Whew!

"Impressive," Siphon says, "but not impressive enough." Then, he creates a giant shadow whip and cracks it at me!

I pull another shadow from beneath the throne and protect myself with a flimsy shadow shield, but Siphon's strike destroys it with one blow. Boy, the way he's fighting you'd think Siphon's been using shadow weapons all his life. But then again, I guess being a Meta 4 gives him even faster mastery of the powers he duplicates.

"Thanks for the save," Night Owl says, running over

and shielding us both with a stronger shadow barrier. "I think we're even now. But if you don't mind me asking, who's the nutso, muscular guy and what's up with the ugly, yellow dude watching this all go down?"

"The yellow guy is Beezle," I say. "He's the evil genie we were looking for. The guy wearing his ring is Siphon, the most dangerous Meta in the entire universe right now. He copies Meta powers so I'm thinking you should get out of here as quickly as possible."

"What?" Night Owl says, blocking another of Siphon's blows. "Are you crazy? I'm not leaving. I've saved you too many times to just let you die. You're like my pet project now."

"Thanks," I say. "But the longer you stay here the more he'll use your powers against us. I need you to grab Haywire and get out of here."

"Haywire?" she says. "Why do we want to help her?"

"Because she's a good person," I say. "She just got herself in over her head. Now go, and make sure you get far away so he can't sense your powers. I'll come up with a plan."

"Like what?" she asks.

"Don't know yet," I answer.

"Well, that's a confidence builder," Night Owl says.

"Thanks," I say. "I'll cover you. Now go!"

Before she can respond, I jump outside her barrier, grab the shadow beneath the roller coaster cars, and push it at Siphon as hard as I can, pinning him to the rock wall.

"I'll be back for you," Night Owl says, shooting me a frustrated look as she jumps on a shadow slide and heads for Haywire.

But just as Night Owl scoops up Haywire, Siphon swipes my own shadow and turns it into a giant hammer, sending it after Night Owl!

"Look out!" I yell.

But just as Night Owl takes off with Haywire in her arms, Siphon's hammer pummels her with a massive blow. Night Owl's body goes limp and she falls to the ground, taking Haywire down with her.

"No one leaves," Siphon says, busting through my shadow barrier. "No one escapes alive. Including you."

Then, he charges at me.

I turn for the stairs and stumble, my hand hitting the podium that controls the ride. I need to protect myself, but as my eyes dart around the room I realize we've used all the shadows in the place. Then, I hear his footsteps behind me and when I turn, I gasp as his big mitt reaches for my neck!

But instead of grabbing me, his hand slows to a stop!

In fact, his entire body has frozen like a statue!

What's going on?

"Hello, Elliott Harkness," comes a familiar voice from behind me.

I turn to find Tormentus standing there with his arms crossed and a devious smile on his face!

What's he doing here?

"My, my," he says, buffing his fingernails. "I'd say you've gotten yourself into quite a bit of trouble."

"D-Did you do this?" I ask. "Did you make him freeze?"

"I did," Tormentus says. "I'm feeling generous today, so given your current circumstances, I thought I'd offer you one last chance to make a deal before you die. And I even have some new terms I think you'll find interesting."

"A-A deal?" I say, totally confused.

"Yes, a deal," Tormentus says. "It's quite a simple one actually. Would you like to hear it?"

"Um, I guess so," I say, cringing as I answer.

"I'll save your life by getting you out of here safe and sound," Tormentus says, "and when you die, I get your soul. Now, I'm rather busy, so I'll give you thirty seconds to decide before I unfreeze your friend here and things go back to being ugly."

Meta Profile

Terrog

⬜ Name: Terrog	⬜ Height: Variable
⬜ Race: Djinn	⬜ Weight: Variable
⬜ Status: Villain/Inactive	⬜ Eyes/Hair: Red/Black

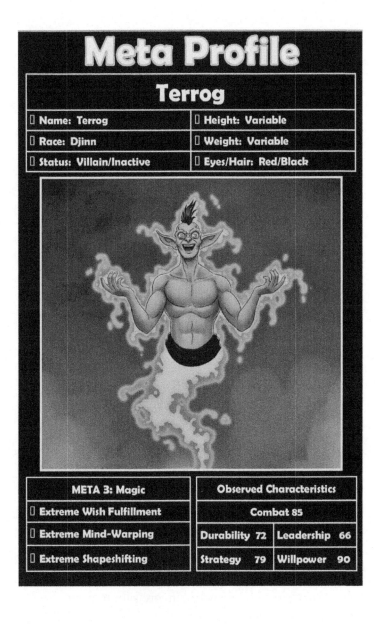

META 3: Magic	Observed Characteristics	
⬜ Extreme Wish Fulfillment	Combat 85	
⬜ Extreme Mind-Warping	Durability 72	Leadership 66
⬜ Extreme Shapeshifting	Strategy 79	Willpower 90

FIFTEEN

I GET MORE THAN I WISHED FOR

Time sure flies when you've got thirty seconds to make the decision of an eternal lifetime.

The way I see it, I'm in a lose-lose situation. Either I sell my soul to Tormentus in exchange for saving my skin, or I tell him to go suck an egg and let Siphon rip me to pieces. Why do I always get myself in these situations?

But as I contemplate my fate, Tormentus just stares at me with a goofy grin on his face. I bet that creep has been waiting for a moment like this. Somehow, he kept tabs on me and swooped in just when I was up against the ropes—exactly like he did to Siphon.

The thing is, Tormentus knows he's got me exactly where he wants me. I mean, Siphon is a Meta 4! The odds of me surviving a battle with him are slim to none.

What to do, what to do?

If I agree to Tormentus' deal, I can get out of here scot-free and live to fight another day. Then, I can regroup and come back with a real plan to stop Siphon. Besides, does anyone really need their soul when they're dead anyway? According to Siphon, Tormentus said he's collecting souls for some kind of war. That sounds ominous, but I guess I wouldn't be around anyway.

But then again, if I take the easy option I'll be leaving Night Owl and Haywire behind. Who knows what Siphon will do to them? Plus, what about Grace? If I can't convince Siphon to bring back the grown-ups then Grace is a goner when she turns fifteen.

Decisions. Decisions.

I look into Tormentus' yellow eyes and wonder if he's trying to influence my thinking like he did at Lockdown. It doesn't seem like he's inside my brain, but it's hard to know for sure so I throw up a little negation field.

"Time's up," Tormentus says, tapping his wrist. "What's it going to be? Will you live, or will you press your luck against this unsophisticated brute?"

Press my luck?

Holy smokes, why didn't I think of that before?

It's a risk, but it's a risk worth taking. Otherwise, I've failed everyone—including myself.

"Well?" Tormentus asks. "What's your answer?"

"Sorry to disappoint," I say, "but I'm going with 'no way Jose!'"

"What?" Tormentus exclaims. "That makes no sense!

As soon as I disappear, time will revert to normal and Siphon will rip you limb from pathetic limb."

"Probably," I say, "but I'd rather do what's right than have my soul spend eternity with a creep like you."

Tormentus' lips curl in anger but I need to act fast because he'll hit the road any second. I turn towards Haywire who is still down for the count. This probably isn't a good idea, but it's the only idea I've got.

"Then you will die a fool!" Tormentus yells, raising his hand to snap his fingers.

I send my duplication powers out and copy as much of Haywire's power as possible. As her Meta energy enters my body, I feel an itchy sensation, like ants are crawling on my skin. But I can't worry about that now, because just as Tormentus SNAPS his fingers and disappears, I spin and project Haywire's power all over Siphon.

Suddenly, Siphon is in motion again and I hit the deck as he trips over his own feet and flies over me, crashing face-first into the rock wall beneath the staircase. It worked! Haywire's bad luck is working on Siphon!

"You're lucky I tripped," Siphon says, getting to his feet. "But your luck has run out."

But then, there's a loud CREAKING noise overhead, and when I look up, the rickety staircase over Siphon collapses, crashing down on top of him! That's when I notice new shadows on the ground beneath the rubble!

Now's my chance!

I project my duplication powers at Night Owl, and as I absorb her power, I make sure I hold onto Haywire's bad luck power. Then, I use Night Owl's power to quickly grab the shadows just as Siphon punches through the debris, sending planks flying everywhere! But as I turn to shield my body I see Beezle floating calmly overhead—and that's when I realize what I need to do.

"Now I'm really annoyed," Siphon says, dusting himself off. But then, he raises his eyebrows and looks frantically from side-to-side. "Who else is here?"

Huh? I don't know what he's talking about, but I'm certainly not going to waste a good opportunity. I form a pair of shadow tongs by his hand and rip the silver ring right off his finger. There's a yellow flash as Beezle gets sucked back into the ring and then a TINGING sound as the ring hits something hard by Siphon's feet.

"The ring!" Siphon yells, dropping to his hands and knees. "Where'd it go?"

"How unlucky," I say, noticing the roller coaster cars behind him. "I don't know where the ring went, but I do know you're going for a ride!"

Then, I create a massive shadow fist and CLOCK him with everything I've got. Siphon flies backward into one of the cars, and as he tumbles inside I convert the shadow fist into an anvil and drop it on him, pinning him down. After that, I make a beeline for the control podium and flick on the ride.

As the roller coaster jolts into operation and takes

Siphon into a tunnel, I race over to grab the ring. But I can't find it! Where'd it go? I've got to find that ring!

But when I kneel, something wet hits my cheek and I'm pushed backward. The next thing I know, a furry dog materializes on top of me.

"Dog-Gone?" I exclaim. "So, that was you Siphon sensed?" As I wrap my arms around him he drops the silver ring into my hands. "And you found the ring! Good boy! For once, I'm glad you didn't listen to me. Now let me up because I've got to end this before Siphon comes back around."

I look at the silver ring in my palm. It's hard to imagine this little ring caused so much craziness. But then again, it's no ordinary ring. I take a deep breath and Dog-Gone whimpers.

"I know," I say, "but it's our only chance."

Then, I put the ring on my finger.

Suddenly, the ring sparks with yellow electricity, and out comes Beezle! He slithers around my body until reaching full size and then looks down with surprise.

"Well, I was not expecting this," he says, "but as you are now the bearer of the silver Ring of Suffering, you are my master and I am at your service."

"Master?" I say. "Don't call me master."

"As you wish, master," Beezle says. "I am here to fulfill your utmost desires. I can grant you three wishes. However, even I have limitations. I am not able to bring the dead back to life and I am not permitted to grant you unlimited wishes. You have three wishes at your disposal, so tell me, what is your desire, master? Perhaps you would like to rule this world?"

"Um, no," I say. "Listen, I'd like—"

"Pardon me, master," Beezle interjects. "But before you speak, I implore you not to be frivolous. After all, you only have three wishes. Let us use them wisely. Let us use them for your benefit, if you know what I mean."

I open my mouth to object but then stop myself. I mean, maybe he's right. Maybe I could use at least one of these wishes to help myself out a bit.

WOOF!

I look down to find Dog-Gone growling at me. Wait a minute, what am I thinking? Beezle is influencing my thinking somehow. I surround myself with negation energy and push Beezle out.

"Master, please?" Beezle pleads.

"Listen, Beezle," I say, "and listen close because I'm making my first wish. I want you to bring back every person Siphon made disappear. All of the grown-ups. All of the teenagers. I want you to put them back exactly as they were when you made them disappear. Got it?"

"Very well, master," Beezle says dryly. And then he waves his hands and two maintenance workers suddenly appear next to the roller coaster track. "Wish fulfilled."

Yes! It worked! So, that means my parents should be back on the Waystation. I'd give anything to go see them, but I'm not done here. Not by a long shot.

"Um, Doug," one of the workers says. "What was in that coffee you gave me? Because if I didn't know better, I'd say I'm looking at the Genie from Aladdin and Superman's dog."

"Same here," Doug says, dropping his tools. "Let's get out of here!"

As they take off, I hear the ROAR of the roller coaster overhead and realize I probably don't have much time until Siphon comes back around. And when he does, he's not going to be happy. There's no way I'll be able to defeat him. In fact, I'm not sure the entire Freedom Force could defeat him. He's just too powerful.

"Beezle, I'd like to make my second wish."

"I cannot wait to hear this one, master," Beezle says.

"I want you to remove Siphon's Meta energy," I say quickly. "All of it, permanently. And fast."

"You said you would like me to remove all of his energy?" Beezle asks, raising his left eyebrow.

Just then, the front of the roller coaster appears in the opposite tunnel. Oh no! Siphon is back!

"Yes!" I answer quickly. "All of it! And do it now!"

"As you wish, master," Beezle says, and then he waves both of his hands. "Wish fulfilled."

I feel an incredible sense of relief as the roller coaster SCREECHES to a halt with Siphon still inside. But while Siphon clearly managed to destroy my shadow anchor, he's slumped over in his seat, not moving. What's going on? Is he knocked out?

Just then, Tormentus appears.

"Wait, what are you doing here?" I ask. "I turned your offer down."

"*You* did," Tormentus says. But then he points to Siphon and says, "But he didn't. And now it's time to collect what is owed to me."

"Collect?" I say, totally confused. But then I realize what he's talking about. He's here for Siphon's soul. B-But that means... "You killed him!" I scream at Beezle.

"Yes, master," Beezle says. "I did as you wished."

"N-No!" I yell. "I-I told you to remove his Meta energy! That's all!"

"Oh, what a shame," Beezle says, covering his mouth with a hand. "I thought I clarified your wish and you desired that I remove his life energy. What a pity."

"You did it on purpose!" I yell. "Bring him back!"

"I cannot do that, master," Beezle says.

"Then I'm using my third wish," I say. "I want you to bring him back from the dead!"

"I am afraid that is not permitted," Beezle says. "I already explained that to you."

"N-No," I say, dropping to my knees.

"I guess there's a lesson here for you," Tormentus says, his eyes glowing white. "When you're working with your enemies the devil is always in the details."

Then, a white mist flows out of Siphon's body and gets sucked into Tormentus' eyes. Tormentus glows bright white as his body temporarily expands. And after he absorbs the last tendrils of Siphon's soul, he shrinks back down to normal size. Then, he looks at me with an evil smile and disappears with a SNAP—leaving Siphon's soulless body behind.

"Epic Zero?"

I feel a hand on my shoulder and look up to see Night Owl standing over me.

"Are you okay?" she asks.

Great question. No, I'm not okay. I never wished for Beezle to kill Siphon. He twisted my words for his own sick purposes. H-He burned me. I'm so overwhelmed with emotion I feel kind of dizzy. But I can't let him do this to anyone, ever again.

"N-Not really," I say, feeling shaky as I get to my feet. "But this ends now. Beezle, I'm making my third wish."

"Of course, master," Beezle says. "Your wish is my command. And now that your greatest enemy is out of our way, perhaps you would like to possess ultimate power? I can grant that for you. I can make you a Meta 4 if that is your desire."

"No, Beezle," I say, "that's not my desire. My desire is really clear so I want you to listen carefully."

"Yes, master," Beezle says. "Of course."

"Excellent," I say. "My wish is for you to go back inside your ring, and never, ever come out again."

"My apologies, master," Beezle says, his voice cracking, "but surely you are joking. There are so many other ways to use your remaining wish. For power. For glory. For—"

"No!" I yell. "That's my third wish and you must obey. After all, I am your master."

"I-I am forced to obey," Beezle says, gritting his teeth. But as he waves his hands, he says, "But beware, my brothers will avennngggeee meeeee…"

And then he disappears into the silver ring.

Suddenly, I hear moaning to our left, and when I turn around Haywire is rolling over slowly. Thank goodness she's okay, but I guess I'll have to tell her about Tormentus and Siphon. After all, her soul is on his collection list.

"Epic Zero!" comes an excited voice.

I look up to see Grace flying towards us with a huge smile on her face. "There you are! I've been looking all over the park for you. You were supposed to call me." Then, she looks around and says. "What the heck happened in here?"

"Long story," I say. Suddenly, I feel really woozy.

"Guess what?" she says, grabbing my shoulders and shaking me. "Mom called me from the Waystation! Mom and Dad are back! The whole team is back! And that means I'm not going to disappear on my birthday!"

"Yeah," I say, my vision fading quickly. I feel like I'm going to… pass out. "Imagine that…"

Then, she let's go of me and I feel myself falling.

And then everything goes dark…

EPILOGUE

I RECEIVE A SURPRISE GIFT

"**H**appy birthday to you!"

After everyone stops singing, Grace makes a wish and blows out fifteen candles on her birthday cake with one breath, proving once and for all that she's full of hot air. But all jokes aside, it's great to see her so happy, even though she had to give up the presidency. And it also feels great to be surrounded by the Freedom Force again. I mean, even Shadow Hawk is smiling!

But Grace's birthday isn't the only thing I have to celebrate, because my parents invited Next Gen and Night Owl to join the party too. I mean, this is a real first. I've never been allowed to have friends on the Waystation before.

I don't know why my parents changed their minds, but I guess they had a lot of time to think about things after Beezle transported them and the other grown-ups to some strange, misty world. My parents said they could see one another through the haze but they couldn't move a muscle. That sounds unbelievably torturous but I'm just glad they're back.

After passing out at Safari Park, I woke up in the Medi-wing and Mom was the first person I saw. We hugged long and hard and I admit I may have even shed a tear or two. Then, Dad gave me a big hug and said to rest up because my body shut down from the stress of saving everyone.

But the thing is, I didn't save everyone.

I still can't shake what happened to Siphon. I know Beezle intentionally misinterpreted my command but it doesn't hurt any less. Siphon was a good kid who was just so misguided. I wish I could have helped him more.

And speaking of wishes, TechnocRat gave his theory on why the Meta Monitor didn't pick up Beezle's signature once he banished the grown-ups. Apparently, Black Magic can only be detected on the things it leaves its trace on. Once my parents and the others were sent away, they took Beezle's power signature with them. That's why the Meta Monitor could read Beezle's signal off the Powerbots because they were still here. TechnocRat said he'll try tweaking the Meta Monitor to fix that, which would be great.

And in other great news, the team reunited Haywire with her parents at the hospital. According to Selfie, Siphon hurt Haywire pretty badly, but now that her parents are back Haywire said she didn't plan on fighting crime anymore. But we'll keep tabs on her anyway, just in case.

Especially if Tormentus pops up again.

The funny thing is, my parents hadn't heard of Tormentus either. I checked again and there's nothing on him in the Meta database. I'll never forget that creep's face. I just hope I never see it again.

"Okay," Mom says, putting a stack of gifts in front of Grace. "Time for presents!"

Presents? Oh no, I never got Grace a present.

"My favorite part!" Grace says, unwrapping the first gift and pulling out a long, white cape. "Wow, a new cape? This is cool."

"That's from me," TechnocRat says, fiddling with his whiskers. "And it's not just any cape. I invented a new polymer to make you more aerodynamic."

"Thanks, T-Rat," she says. "That's so thoughtful. Okay, I'll open this one next." She opens up a small box and pulls out a gift card. "Whoa! That's a lot of cash!"

"That's from Blue Bolt, Makeshift, Master Mime, and me," Shadow Hawk says. "We thought you could redecorate your bedroom."

"Now that you're a sophisticated young lady, of course," Blue Bolt adds with a curtsy.

"Of course," Grace says with a smile. "Gee, thanks. That's amazing. Okay, I'll do this one next." Then, she tears it open and pulls out a new phone. "Really?" she says, hugging it and looking at Mom and Dad. "You got me the latest model? How did you know I wanted one?"

"Gee, I don't know," Mom says slyly. "It's not like I could read your mind or anything."

"Happy birthday, dear," Dad says.

I look at the pile and see two presents left. One is large and neatly wrapped, while the other is small and looks like it was wrapped by a rabid raccoon.

"I'll open this one," Grace says, carefully picking up the small one. But as she unwraps it, a bone falls out and THUNKS onto the table.

"Wow," Grace says. "Dog-Gone, is this from you?"

Dog-Gone appears, picks up the bone, and then disappears.

"Um, okay," Grace says. "You play with it first."

Great. Even Dog-Gone got her a present.

Ugh! Now she's opening the last one and she'll know I got her nothing! I wish I could disappear like Dog-Gone.

"Just one more," she says, looking at me. "It's a big one too. Yum, this one smells good." And when she unwraps it her eyes light up with surprise. "It's two dozen jelly doughnuts!"

"That's from all of us in Next Gen," Selfie says, "including Epic Zero."

What? Really? I look over at Selfie and she smiles.

"Thanks, guys," she says, grabbing a doughnut and taking a huge bite. "Yah know," she says, talking with her mouth full, "you guyth aren't tho bad."

"Okay, let's eat," Mom says, using her telekinesis to start cutting the cake.

"Thanks for the save," I whisper to Selfie.

"We're a team, right?" she whispers back with a wink. "Besides, I figured you weren't exactly in a state to get her anything."

"By the way," Night Owl says, "when Selfie said that gift was from *all* of us in Next Gen, she meant *all* of us, including me."

"Wait, what?" I say. "Are you joining the team?"

"Yeah," she says. "Like Glory Girl said, you guys aren't so bad. Besides, I could get used to hanging around a place like this."

"That's awesome!" I say.

"Anyone else notice we're being taken over by girls?" Pinball asks, taking a giant bite of cake. "I kinda like it."

"Epic Zero," Dad says, "can we see you for a minute?"

"Um, sure," I say. And suddenly I have a feeling of dread. The last conversation I had with my parents was about disbanding Next Gen. Is that why they invited them? Is this our last hurrah?

"Um, what's up?" I say, meeting them in the corner.

"We just wanted to tell you we're proud of you,"

Dad says. "Really proud of you."

"Really?" I say.

"Yes," Mom says. "And we see you've taken our leadership lessons to heart."

"I-I did?" I say.

"Yes," Dad says. "Grace told us you protected your team from danger because you recognized they couldn't handle Haywire, and that's the sign of a great leader."

"Thanks," I say, totally floored.

"But that's not all," Mom says. "Your father and I agreed that you should continue leading Next Gen."

"Wait, what?" I say. "You mean we don't have to disband?"

"No," Dad says. "In fact, we'd like the Freedom Force to help mentor you—all of you. If you're going to be the next generation of heroes, then let's train you to do it the right way."

"Seriously?" I say. "That's amazing! Wait until I tell the team!"

"Absolutely," Mom says, "but let's celebrate your sister for today. After all, she's only fifteen once."

"Right," I say, turning to see Grace showing Night Owl her new cape.

Even though I'm bursting with excitement, I'm happy to wait to share the news. I still can't believe what my parents said. I mean, now we'll really have a chance to become a great superhero team. We'll be able to fight major bad guys, and who knows, we might end up collecting a few trophies of our own.

Speaking of trophies, Grace said she put the silver Ring of Suffering back in the Trophy Room next to the bronze one. But that still leaves the gold ring unaccounted for. I look out the porthole towards Earth, wondering where it could be.

"Epic Zero!" Pinball shouts, snapping me back to reality. "Come on! Makeshift is giving us a tour of the Waystation. Did you know there's an Evacuation Chamber that actually shoots dog poo into space?"

Okay, so maybe it'll take us a while to become a great superhero team, but I know one thing, I'm ready for the journey!

EPIC ZERO 8 IS AVAILABLE NOW!

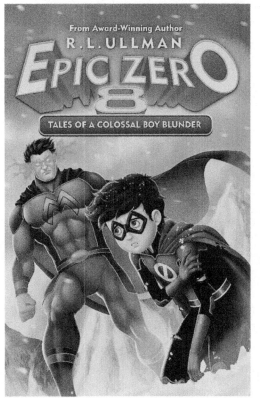

Before the Freedom Force, the Protectors of the Planet were the greatest Meta team of their time, until they were betrayed by one of their own leading to tragedy. Now, Meta-Man, the most powerful hero of them all, has returned for revenge against his former teammates—and only Elliott can stop him!

Get EPIC ZERO 8:
Tales of a Colossal Boy Blunder today!

YOU CAN MAKE A BIG DIFFERENCE

Calling all heroes! I need your help to get Epic Zero 7 in front of more readers.

Reviews are extremely helpful in getting attention for my books. I wish I had the marketing muscle of the major publishers, but instead, I have something far more valuable, loyal readers, just like you! Your generosity in providing an honest review will help bring this book to the attention of more readers.

So, if you've enjoyed this book, I would be very grateful if you could spare a minute to leave a review on the book's Amazon page. Thanks for your support!

Stay Epic!

R.L. Ullman

META POWERS GLOSSARY

FROM THE META MONITOR:

There are nine known Meta power classifications. These classifications have been established to simplify Meta identification and provide a quick framework to understand a Meta's potential powers and capabilities. **Note:** Metas can possess powers in more than one classification. In addition, Metas can evolve over time in both the powers they express, as well as the effectiveness of their powers.

Due to the wide range of Meta abilities, superpowers have been further segmented into power levels. Power levels differ across Meta power classifications. In general, the following power levels have been established:

- Meta 0: Displays no Meta power.
- Meta 1: Displays limited Meta power.
- Meta 2: Displays considerable Meta power.
- Meta 3: Displays extreme Meta power.

The following is a brief overview of the nine Meta power classifications.

ENERGY MANIPULATION:

Energy Manipulation is the ability to generate, shape, or act as a conduit, for various forms of energy. Energy Manipulators can control energy by focusing or redirecting energy towards a specific target or shaping/reshaping energy for a specific task. Energy Manipulators are often impervious to the forms of energy they can manipulate.

Examples of the types of energies utilized by Energy Manipulators include, but are not limited to:

- Atomic
- Chemical
- Cosmic
- Electricity
- Gravity
- Heat
- Light
- Magnetic
- Sound
- Space
- Time

Note: the fundamental difference between an Energy Manipulator and a Meta-morph with Energy Manipulation capability is that an Energy Manipulator does not change their physical, molecular state to either generate or transfer energy (see META-MORPH).

FLIGHT:
Flight is the ability to fly, glide, or levitate above the Earth's surface without the use of an external source (e.g. jetpack). Flight can be accomplished through a variety of methods, these include, but are not limited to:

- Reversing the forces of gravity
- Riding air currents
- Using planetary magnetic fields
- Wings

Metas exhibiting Flight can range from barely sustaining flight a few feet off the ground to reaching the far limits of outer space.

Often, Metas with Flight ability also display the complementary ability of Super-Speed. However, it can be difficult to decipher if Super-Speed is a Meta power in its own right or is simply a function of combining the Meta's Flight ability with the Earth's natural gravitational force.

MAGIC:
Magic is the ability to display a wide variety of Meta abilities by channeling the powers of a secondary magical or mystical source. Known secondary sources of Magic powers include, but are not limited to:

- Alien lifeforms
- Dark arts
- Demonic forces
- Departed souls
- Mystical spirits

Typically, the forces of Magic are channeled through an enchanted object. Known magical, enchanted objects include:

- Amulets
- Books
- Cloaks
- Gemstones
- Wands

- Weapons

Some Magicians can transport themselves into the mystical realm of their magical source. They may also have the ability to transport others into and out of these realms as well.

Note: the fundamental difference between a Magician and an Energy Manipulator is that a Magician typically channels their powers from a mystical source that likely requires the use of an enchanted object to express these powers (see ENERGY MANIPULATOR).

META MANIPULATION:
Meta Manipulation is the ability to duplicate or negate the Meta powers of others. Meta Manipulation is a rare Meta power and can be extremely dangerous if the Meta Manipulator is capable of manipulating the powers of multiple Metas at one time. Meta Manipulators who can manipulate the powers of several Metas at once have been observed to reach Meta 4 power levels.

Based on the unique powers of the Meta Manipulator, it is hypothesized that other abilities could include altering or controlling the powers of others. Despite their tremendous abilities, Meta Manipulators are often unable to generate powers of their own and are limited to manipulating the powers of others. When not utilizing their abilities, Meta Manipulators may be vulnerable to attack.

Note: It has been observed that a Meta Manipulator requires close physical proximity to a Meta target to fully manipulate their power. When fighting a Meta

Manipulator, it is advised to stay at a reasonable distance and to attack from long range. Meta Manipulators have been observed manipulating the powers of others up to 100 yards away.

META-MORPH:
Meta-morph is the ability to display a wide variety of Meta abilities by "morphing" all, or part, of one's physical form from one state into another. There are two sub-types of Meta-morphs:

- Physical
- Molecular

Physical morphing occurs when a Meta-morph transforms their physical state to express their powers. Physical Meta-morphs typically maintain their human physiology while exhibiting their powers (with the exception of Shapeshifters). Types of Physical morphing include, but are not limited to:

- Invisibility
- Malleability (elasticity/plasticity)
- Physical by-products (silk, toxins, etc...)
- Shapeshifting
- Size changes (larger or smaller)

Molecular morphing occurs when a Meta-morph transforms their molecular state from a normal physical state to a non-physical state to express their powers. Types of Molecular morphing include, but are not limited to:

- Fire
- Ice
- Rock
- Sand
- Steel
- Water

Note: Because Meta-morphs can display abilities that mimic all other Meta power classifications, it can be difficult to properly identify a Meta-morph upon the first encounter. However, it is critical to carefully observe how their powers manifest, and, if it is through Physical or Molecular morphing, you can be certain you are dealing with a Meta-morph.

PSYCHIC:
Psychic is the ability to use one's mind as a weapon. There are two sub-types of Psychics:

- Telepaths
- Telekinetics

Telepathy is the ability to read and influence the thoughts of others. While Telepaths often do not appear to be physically intimidating, their power to penetrate minds can often result in more devastating damage than a physical assault.

Telekinesis is the ability to manipulate physical objects with one's mind. Telekinetics can often move objects with their mind that are much heavier than they could move physically. Many Telekinetics can also make objects move at very high speeds.

Note: Psychics are known to strike from long distance, and, in a fight, it is advised to incapacitate them as quickly as possible. Psychics often become physically drained from the extended use of their powers.

SUPER-INTELLIGENCE:

Super-Intelligence is the ability to display levels of intelligence above standard genius intellect. Super-Intelligence can manifest in many forms, including, but not limited to:

- Superior analytical ability
- Superior information synthesizing
- Superior learning capacity
- Superior reasoning skills

Note: Super-Intellects continuously push the envelope in the fields of technology, engineering, and weapons development. Super-Intellects are known to invent new approaches to accomplish previously impossible tasks. When dealing with a Super-Intellect, you should be mentally prepared to face challenges that have never been encountered before. In addition, Super-Intellects can come in all shapes and sizes. The most advanced Super-Intellects have originated from non-human creatures.

SUPER-SPEED:

Super-Speed is the ability to display movement at remarkable physical speeds above standard levels of speed. Metas with Super-Speed often exhibit complementary abilities to movement that include, but are not limited to:

- Enhanced endurance
- Phasing through solid objects
- Super-fast reflexes
- Time travel

Note: Metas with Super-Speed often have an equally super metabolism, burning thousands of calories per minute, and requiring them to eat many extra meals a day to maintain consistent energy levels. It has been observed that Metas exhibiting Super-Speed are quick thinkers, making it difficult to keep up with their thought process.

SUPER-STRENGTH:

Super-Strength is the ability to utilize muscles to display remarkable levels of physical strength above expected levels of strength. Metas with Super-Strength can lift or push objects that are well beyond the capability of an average member of their species. Metas exhibiting Super-Strength can range from lifting objects twice their weight to incalculable levels of strength allowing for the movement of planets.

Metas with Super-Strength often exhibit complementary abilities to strength that include, but are not limited to:

- Earthquake generation through stomping
- Enhanced jumping
- Invulnerability
- Shockwave generation through clapping

Note: Metas with Super-Strength may not always possess this strength evenly. Metas with Super-Strength have been observed to demonstrate powers in only one arm or leg.

META PROFILE CHARACTERISTICS

FROM THE META MONITOR:

In addition to having a strong working knowledge of a Meta's powers and capabilities, it is also imperative to understand the key characteristics that form the core of their character. When facing or teaming up with Metas, understanding their key characteristics will help you gain deeper insight into their mentality and strategic potential.

What follows is a brief explanation of the five key characteristics you should become familiar with. **Note:** the data that appears in each Meta profile has been compiled from live field activity.

COMBAT:

The ability to defeat a foe in hand-to-hand combat.

DURABILITY:

The ability to withstand significant wear, pressure, or damage.

LEADERSHIP:

The ability to lead a team of disparate personalities and powers to victory.

STRATEGY:

The ability to find, and successfully exploit, a foe's weakness.

WILLPOWER:

The ability to persevere, despite seemingly insurmountable odds.

ABOUT THE AUTHOR

R.L. Ullman is the bestselling author of the award-winning EPIC ZERO series and the award-winning MONSTER PROBLEMS series. He creates fun, engaging page-turners that captivate the imaginations of kids and adults alike. His original, relatable characters face adventure and adversity that bring out their inner strengths. He's frequently distracted thinking up new stories, and once got lost in his own neighborhood. You can learn more about what R.L. is up to at rlullman.com, and if you see him wandering around your street please point him in the right direction home.

ACKNOWLEDGMENTS

Without the support of these brave heroes, I would have been trampled by supervillains before I could bring this series to print. I would like to thank my wife, Lynn (a.k.a. Mrs. Marvelous); my son Matthew (a.k.a. Captain Creativity); my daughter Olivia (a.k.a. Ms. Positivity); and my furry sidekicks Howie and Sadie. I would also like to thank all of the readers out there who have connected with Elliott and his amazing family. Stay Epic!